Killers on Elm Street

Romell Tukes

Lock Down Publications and Ca$h
Presents

Killers on Elm Street

A Novel by *Romell Tukes*

Romell Tukes

Lock Down Publications
P.O. Box 944
Stockbridge, Ga 30281
www.lockdownpublications.com

Copyright 2021 Romell Tukes
Killers on Elm Street

First Edition March 2021
Printed in the United States of America

Lock Down Publications
Like our page on Facebook: Lock Down Publications @
www.facebook.com/lockdownpublications.ldp
Cover design and layout by: **Dynasty Cover Me**
Book interior design by: **Shawn Walker**
Edited by: **Jill Alicea**

Stay Connected with Us!

Text **LOCKDOWN** to 22828 to stay up-to-date with new releases, sneak peaks, contests and more...

Thank you!

Submission Guideline.

Submit the first three chapters of your completed manuscript to ldpsubmissions@gmail.com, subject line: Your book's title. The manuscript must be in a .doc file and sent as an attachment. Document should be in Times New Roman, double spaced and in size 12 font. Also, provide your synopsis and full contact information. If sending multiple submissions, they must each be in a separate email.

Have a story but no way to send it electronically? You can still submit to LDP/Ca$h Presents. Send in the first three chapters, written or typed, of your completed manuscript to:

LDP: Submissions Dept
P.O. Box 944
Stockbridge, Ga 30281

DO NOT send original manuscript. Must be a duplicate.

Provide your synopsis and a cover letter containing your full contact information.

Thanks for considering LDP and Ca$h Presents.

Acknowledgments

First and foremost, all praises are due to Allah. Shout to all the loyal readers, I got you. Shout to my family. Shout to Yonkers, NY, and the whole 914, Peeky and MV. Shout to Moreno aka Smoke, love you, bro. Shout Killer from Peeky, Spice from Newbury, CB, YB, Lingo, Chop, Banger, Baby James, Brisco da Makk, Red, PC, and the whole Y.O. Bama got us! We litty! Shout my BX fam, Melly da Makk and Roll out aka Ro Bolla, Frillz, Murda from Little Rock, and B.G., Beast, and Rugar from Patterson, NJ. Shout my BK goons, OG Chuck, Tom Dog, Rio, Day, Green Eye, Gunny, and Tails from Crown Heights. Shout my D.C. niggas, Lee from Uptown, La-La from Lincoln Heights 50th N.E., and H-Mob from S.E. Big shout to Lock Down Publications, the game is ours Stay tuned it's a move, you heard!!!

Romell Tukes

Chapter 1

Manhattan, NY

Wolf was seated in his Criminal Justice class at NYU college listening to his professor go over an old case, Strickland v. the United States.

"You want to meet up at study hall to go over this before Tuesday's quiz?" a beautiful Spanish woman asked Wolf when the class was over, and everybody started to leave.

"I can't today, Bella. My sister wanted me to come to her basketball game. It's the last one of the season," Wolf told Bella, placing his laptop into his backpack.

"Oh, I saw her on the news last week. She's ranked as the number one female high school point guards in New York," Bella said, following him out of the class and into the packed halls full of loud college students.

"Yeah, she got seven D-1 colleges on her body right now, but she told me that she's feeling LSU."

"That's a good look. But why you ain't call me last night, nigga?" Bella said, giving him an evil look.

"My bad, ma. I forgot. After studying for three hours, I was finished," he replied, walking into the school parking lot. He noticed that the sun was going down because two hours ago it was close to one hundred degrees outside.

"You got a pass this time, Papi. But you still coming to seaside with us in New Jersey for that party," Bella said, stopping at his black BMW 7 Series 750i with peanut butter interior and black tints with rims.

"I thought you said everybody wanted to go to Webster Hall?" Wolf said, placing his backpack in his backseat.

"Ewwww. Hell no. That shit is too ratchet, Romeo. Most of us are about to be a part of the police force, so we're not trying to risk our careers or our lives at a club full of wannabe thugs, fighting and shooting," she said, seriously.

"Since I am going to be a lawyer, I can help you get out of jail. However, I am going to charge you a fee," he said, looking at her curves in her low-cut jeans.

"Boy, whatever. Call me later so we can go over this exam."

"Where you going?"

"To the study hall to study. Tell your sister that I said hey," Bella said, walking off back into the school.

Wolf and Bella had been close friends since they started their freshman year almost four years ago. They both graduated from high school at the age of sixteen years old and majored in Criminal Justice at New York University.

Wolf made his way to the nearby highway heading home to the slums of Yonkers, New York. It was a forty-minute drive from where his college was located.

Wolf's real name was Romeo Veldez. He was Black and Dominican. His mom was Black and his father, who he never saw, was Dominican. He was six-one in height, brown skin, brown and green eyes, short and wavy slick hair with a taper, lean, and handsome. Born and raised in Yonkers was rough for him, especially on Elm Street where the crime rate was at an all-time high. He had two older brothers, one was in state prison for a murder and his other brother was a known bank robber.

Wolf was always a very smart kid and always on the honor roll in school. He dreamed of being a lawyer to help others fight cases and give his Black people a fair chance. He saw so many niggas that he grew up with getting railroaded by the injustice court system.

His sister, Victoria, was his pride and joy. She was eighteen years old with her head on her shoulders correctly. She was one of the best basketball players in the state and she worked hard to get where she wanted to be in life. Wolf taught her how to play basketball at the age of eleven and she had been a problem since then.

***

Roosevelt High School
Yonkers, NY

Victoria was running up and down the court banging out layups. The game was in the 4th quarter and her team was up by twenty points. The score was 32 – 52 and Victoria put up 36 points all by herself, which was normal.

Every game she avenged over thirty points and seven to nine assists; she was hands down a female Kobe. That was her nickname in school because she brought the same intensity. With this being her last year she turned it up a notch. She graduated in less than three months and then she would pick her college where she would attend.

Victoria was a young beauty, high yellow, Spanish features, short, long thick jet-black hair, a nice petite frame, and greenish eyes. She and Wolf had different fathers, but they still had similar feathers.

"Vic come sit out. We got two minutes left on the clock. Come on!" her coach yelled, subbing her out for another player because she was already there.

The school gym was full of students, friends, and family members. The gym was so loud, Victoria couldn't hear herself think. She hated it when this happened.

She looked into the audience to see Wolf in the crowd winking at her as she smiled back. Her brother was her life. He was like the father that she never had. Their mother, Rita, did everything she could to keep a roof over their head by working two jobs. Victoria had two other brothers, Black and CB. CB was in prison and Black lived in the Bronx, so all she had was Wolf.

The buzzer rang and the game was over. Her team won. She started jumping around and cheering with the crowd.

"You was looking like MJ out there," Wolf said, sneaking up behind Victoria talking to a group of chicks.

"Brother!" she screamed, jumping into his arms.

"You did good," Wolf said.

"She stole the game," another ballplayer said.

"Don't be hating," Victoria said, laughing.

"You drove up here?" Wolf asked.

"Yeah, but I'm about to leave. Let me grab my bag," Victoria said, racing off and leaving her friends staring at Wolf

"She wants to know if you got a girlfriend. Well, we all do," one of the girls said, blushing.

Wolf walked off without saying a word. He was twenty-one years old. He was a grown man and he only dealt with grown women.

"We out," Victoria said, leading the way out to the parking lot filled with cars trying to get out.

"How was college today?" Victoria asked, seeing how dark it was outside.

"Cool, I guess. Bella said hey."

"Uhmm, I like her. I can't believe you never hit that. She's fire. A nigga going cuff that one day and she about to be a cop. Bro, you lacking," she said, walking behind her Acura.

"That's her!" a nigga said, pulling up to them in a navy-blue Toyota Avalon with three niggas in the car ice grilling them both.

Wolf felt the stares and he knew something was wrong.

BOC! BOC! BOC! BOC! BOC! BOC! BOC! BOC! BOC!

The men in the Toyota hit Victoria six times in her stomach and Wolf twice in his leg. A nigga wearing a hoodie came to Wolf out of nowhere, firing shots at the Toyota and killing the nigga in the back seat.

BOOM! BOOM! BOOM! BOOM! BOOM!

The shooter shot out the Toyota's back windows as it raced out the parking lot.

The shooter caught eye contact with Wolf, who was holding Victoria. Civilians called the police as students screamed and cried when they saw who it was on the floor in a puddle of blood.

The gunman ran off with his hoodie on when he heard sirens coming up the street.

Wolf cried holding Victoria in his arms. She was gasping for air, trying to say she loved him.

When the police and EMS workers got there, they went to work trying to save her life.

***

Hours Later
St. Joseph Hospital

Wolf walked out of the ICU double doors with a cast on his left leg and a cane in his hand. Luckily, the two bullets went through his legs, so his injury wasn't major at all.

"Baby, oh my God! You're okay!" his mom, Rita, yelled, hugging him with puffy eyes." I've been here two hours and the doctors said Vic is on life support, but they're working on her," Rita said, sitting down.

"I know. It's okay. She will pull through. Mom, let's pray," Wolf said, bowing his head with his mom.

After twenty more minutes of waiting, two doctors came out with a clipboard.

"Mrs. Jackson?" the black female asked.

"Yes!" Rita jumped up

"I'm so sorry. Your daughter didn't make it."

"Noooo… not my baby…. Please, Lord, don't take my baby," Rita cried, falling on her knees. Wolf went to help his mom as he was also shedding tears for the loss of his sister.

Romell Tukes

Chapter 2

Sleepy Hollow, NY
Meanwhile

Champ rode in the gray Toyota with a body in the trunk. His little cousin, Fred, was tailing him in a white hooptie. The car made a left off the highway, down a small road leading into a lake in the dark wooded area. Champ used to come here as a kid to go fishing with his father before he died of cancer.

Champ was a known killer and drug dealer from Yonkers. He was thirty-three years old with a long rap sheet. He recently came home from doing a bid up north for an attempt murder charge.

With two kids and a wife at home, most men would come home to stay home, but Champ was different. He loved violence and drama like jail niggas loved commissary. He was nothing like his younger brother, Ling Loa, who was in the FEDs for gang violence and gun charges. His little brother was a crazy hothead with no type of sense and the only thing on his mind was Crippin.

Champ parked next to a ditch, ready to bury his little cousin who got caught in the crossfire. He didn't want Lil Ease to go on the mission in the first place. He was only nineteen years old with no shooting experience, but his brother, Fred, convinced Champ to bring him along.

Champ knew who the mystery shooter was in the hoodie. He knew his face from anywhere because he was fucking Champ's ex-bitch who left Champ in prison for him. When Champ saw Andy shooting at him, blood rushed his brains. The two men had words back and forth on social media, but nothing too crazy because it was all over a bitch.

"We have to be quick. Start digging over there," Champ told Fred, who looked like he'd been crying.

"Nigga get it together. I told you from the jump not to bring him!" Champ yelled, popping the trunk to see Lil Ease's bloody, stiff, and smelly body.

"I know, but that doesn't change the fact that he's my brother," Fred said with two shovels in his hands. He walked over to the grassy area where Champ pointed to start digging.

"Soft ass nigga," Champ whispered to himself while grabbing Lil Ease's body out the trunk and dragging him over to where Fred was digging.

Both men were tall and very muscular, it was in their genes. Fred was digging away while Champ just stood there pacing, thinking if they shot the right person because it was dark outside in the high school parking lot.

"Nigga, you plan on helping, son?"

"He's not my brother," Champ replied, making Fred shake his head while he dug for over an hour. When the hole was deep enough, Champ tossed Lil Ease's body inside and covered it with dirt.

"You did a good job tonight, Fred. I'm proud of you, cuz, but don't mention nothing to nobody or our lives will be over. I know you like to pillow talk, son," Champ said.

"Come on, Champ. You know I'm solid. But what am I supposed to tell mommy? Her son disappeared? Ran off with a white chick? What?"

"I don't know, find something. Tell her he went to Atlanta," Champ said not really caring as long as his name wasn't in the mix. They're eventually gonna find his body, but until then, play it cool, bro," Champ said, walking to the Toyota.

"A'ight. I got you," Fred said, wiping the sweat from his forehead.

"You brought the gasoline and shit?"

"Yeah," Fred said, passing him the gas container out the back seat of the Buick.

Champ poured gas all over the car before throwing a match on the Toyota watching it come to life in flames.

"Beautiful…" Champ said, grinning while Fred looked at him in disbelief. Fred and Champ were both the same age and grew up together. Over the years, Champ mentally worsened.

They hopped in the Buick and drove off back to Yonkers to a neighborhood called Riverdale.

***

Queens, NY

Andy watched two beautiful, exotic, thick Spanish women slide up and down the pole on the stage behind the bar in Club Angel. He was seated in the back by himself in a small section drinking D'usse out of the glass bottle. Tonight, he needed to get outta Yonkers, especially after what happened last night at the high school. He went to school with Victoria before he dropped out two years ago and she was cool people. He thought that she was the baddest bitch in the school.

He saw Champ creep into the parking lot looking for someone. At first, he thought it was him because he cuffed his old bitch. When he saw him shoot Victoria, he had to do something because Andy knew she was an innocent girl with a bright future.

Andy knew for a fact he shot someone in the Toyota. He only hoped it was Champ.

Andy was a stick-up kid from Yonkers in a section called Elm Street where the city's dangerous killers reside. He was twenty years old, Black male with smooth dark skin. He was a tall nigga with a slim build, short hair that had the waves swimming in circles. He had chinky eyes, tattoos on his face and body, along with a small cut on the left side of his face from a knife fight four years ago.

Growing up, his mom died giving birth to his little sister in the hospital, so his grandma and father, Big Bruce, raised him. Andy had so much beef all throughout New York because he would go to different areas to rob whoever was getting money.

Andy saw one of the baddest bitches in the club approach him in a one-piece bikini with fishnets under. The dancer was a Dominican woman. She was thick with a big ass that was round and soft. She had a flat stomach, big breasts, and long goldish hair, with long fake eyelashes but she was beautiful with her golden complexion.

"Andy," she said slow dancing in front of him, but he looked past her into the stage surrounded by thirsty niggas throwing money.

"What's up Shantell? I ain't know you worked in here tonight. If I did, I wouldn't have come," Andy said, looking into her brown eyes and not even glazing at her body which was a piece of art.

"Boy, shut up," she said, dancing to a Daddy Yankee song.

"What's up? Why you all out here?" he said to her.

"You see them four Jamaicans in the VIP corner?"

"Yeah," Andy said because he was watching them toss a lot of money and buy the bar out. All the jewelry they had on is what really caught his attention.

"They're from Mount Vernon. They move a lot of weed and pills, a lot," she said in a low pitch voice, turning around to shake her ass.

"Shantell, I don't want to see that shit," Andy said.

"Nigga, chill. I have to make it look good, Papi," she said, turning back around.

"I'm on it. Thank you. Send this to Smurf," he said, passing his boy's girlfriend two hundred dollars.

"Nigga, you wish you had a bitch with all this ass," she said, walking off. Shantell was from Yonkers. She was his best friend's wifey. They had all grown up together. She would put him on licks sometimes when big spenders would come through. She was a grimy Dominican bitch.

Andy watched the Jamaicans all night spend close to a quarter-million dollars in the club. When they left with dancers, he left with them keeping a distant hoping tonight would be a good night.

Chapter 3

Mount Vernon, NY

Zion whipped the black Cadillac Escalade SUV into the 24/7 gas station to buy some Newport 100's cigarettes and Backwood to roll his trees in because the night was just the beginning. He had two dark-skin strippers in the truck with big asses but ugly faces, they begged him to take them with him for the nightcap and he was down for a threesome.

Zion approached the Denali truck behind him full of his goons and he told them to go home for the night. He would holler at them in the morning. Once his guards pulled off, he ran into the store and got what he needed.

Mount Vernon was next door to the city of Yonkers, but Mount Vernon was mainly West Indians and Jamaicans. Zion was a big connect for exotic weed and ecstasy pills. His family in Kingston, Jamaica was reputed to have been down with the infamous Shower Posse, a notorious drug gang formed in the '80s, so they made sure he was good.

At forty years old, he looked very young. He had dark skin like Flavor Flav and was just as ugly with long skinny dreads that touched the floor with his five-six height.

Zion lived down the street from where the old school rapper Heavy D grew up. He had a new mini-mansion with a small wrap around driveway. The lushly manicured landscape was perfect. The mind-blowing mansion had six bedrooms, four bathrooms, a game room, a pool hall, a gourmet kitchen, a pub room with a full bar, a walk-in cooler, and a safe.

"Ladies," Zion said, letting the women into his home to see their facial expressions.

"Damn, nigga, you got money! A bitch gotta suck that dick good tonight," one of the women said.

"Shit gurl, I'm gonna suck the shit out this nigga's ass," the other women said, licking her huge lips.

"Nah, I ain't doing all that. I got kids to kiss," the other dancer said seriously.

"Have a seat, nuh werry. Me got coke, trees, and drink for yah," Zion said.

"We want all of that and molly," one of them said as he walked off to get the women in the mood. The women took off their heels and dresses while leaving on their thongs, which left their flat and saggy breasts hanging freely.

"Guinness," he offered them.

"Yeah," they both said, accepting the beers. Zion then pulled out three Ziploc bags from under his chair, placing it on the living room table. The table was full of coke, weed, and molly.

"Hell yeah," one of the women said, starting the party. The women started to sniff thick lines of coke and Zion rolled up his weed. He didn't sniff shit up his nose.

"Let me get a taste of that meat, daddy," the dancer with the large lips said, walking over to Zion who was sitting in a La-Z-Boy chair and blowing weed smoke in the air.

She pulled his dick out of his Balmain skinny jeans and went in for the kill. Slowly, she took him in and out her watery mouth.

"Mmmmmmm…." he moaned, watching her head bob up and down on his dick until he shot a load in her mouth. She slurped it up and played with his cum, but didn't swallow it. She had too much class for that. "Let's take this show to the bedroom," Zion demanded until he heard his front door kick open.

Zion tried to reach for his pistol on the living room table, but was too slow. Andy shot him in his right arm.

"Ahhhahhh bumbaclot!" Zion screamed in serious pain, grabbing his arm. The two dancers were so high, they didn't know what to do except stare with confusion.

"Where is it? I want everything!"

"Me have nuttin, mon," he shouted.

"Okay."

Bloc! Bloc! Bloc! Bloc!

Andy killed both dancers, then aimed his Glock 17 with a thirty-shot-clip back at Zion, letting him know that he meant business.

"It's in the walk-in cooler safe. The code is 13-7-16," Zion gritted out. He was looking into his face trying to see if he knew him, but the face didn't click.

"Good looking, son."

"Hold on I..."

Bloc! Bloc! Bloc! Bloc!

Andy fired bullets into his neck and face, silencing him for good.

Andy found a walk-in cooler on the other side of the house. He saw a large safe with a digital keypad. When he punched the numbers in, the safe opened slowly. When he saw pounds of weed and pills with stacks of money underneath, his heart raced. Everything was stacked up at least five feet high.

He ran to the closet to find luggage bags and he started to fill up the bag at a fast pace. It took him thirteen minutes to fill seven bags and then he got the fuck out of there.

This was the first time Shantell put him on a real official lick and he planned to break her off part of the loot for doing so. He had a couple of little cousins who sold pills and weed, so he planned to hit their hand also.

***

Five Point Maximum Prison

"Yo son, wake up. They about to call night rec, ahkee," Smurf yelled to his celly, Snap, who was a Muslim from Brooklyn serving a twenty-four-year bid for two attempt murders and an armed robbery.

"Nah, son. I'ma stay back and pray then go back to sleep. You had a nigga in the town all day with your flicks you heard, I'm tired, boy," Snap said, laying in his bunk.

"A'ight I'ma go hit this yard and holler at the homie. Your little man was supposed to shoot a Crip nigga who just pulled up from Brooklyn. I'm trying to see this movie," Smurf said, getting dressed in his red Champion sweatsuit and butter Timbs as if he was about to hit the block.

"I saw enough movies in this joint."

"You got the hammer," Smurf asked Snap, who pulled out a ten-inch ice pick from under his pillow. Both men stayed strapped and on point, especially being in a maximum-security prison behind the wall. Smurf was a Blood gang member and Snap was a devoted gangsta Muslim.

"I'll be back on the early go back," Smurf said as all the doors unlocked on his block 11-B.

Smurf walked through the hallways in a single file line. He nodded his head at a couple of Blood niggas he knew and niggas from Yonkers he dealt with like his right-hand, Moreno.

Smurf's real name was Sean Lambert. He is from Yonkers on Elm Street. He's twenty-two years old, medium height, light skin, short dreads, handsome with a thick beard, and a loud personality.

He caught a three-year bid for a robbery he did with his best friend, Andy, who got away. They both got caught at the scene robbing a drug dealer in a corner store around the corner from a police station.

Smurf made himself get caught by falling, so Andy could get away. Both men were like brothers since the first grade. Since he'd been down, Andy had been setting him up with money, books, magazines, thirty-five-pound food packages, pics, and whatever he needed. He also looked out for Shantell, who was his rider since day one. Even though he had another chick, she was always number one.

He had no issue with her dancing since that was her hustle. She told him everything, even when she did her thing, but he didn't care because he was in jail. She visited him daily and played her role, so he was cool.

Everybody was outside posted on the wall looking at a big stocky Crip nigga on the yard phone. In a fast motion, a short kid in a hoodie spits a razor out his mouth so fast. He ended up cutting the Crip in his face and passed the razor to a Blood leaning on the wall as the Crip nigga ran to the C.O. for medical attention. This was every day up top because the Bloods run the jails.

Chapter 4

Jersey City, NJ

"Black, are you sure you want to do this shit today? I mean two guards are posted right at the entrance," Styles stated, looking across the street at the Bank of America on the busy main street.

"That's very contemplative and thoughtful of you. But if you're scared, get a dog. We have to go in here with a strong cerebral mental state or you will fail, and deficiency isn't in my plans. You're my bro. I didn't put the gun to your head and tell you to come on this mission with me, did I?" Black asked with a corrosive sarcasm.

Black met Styles seven years ago when he moved to Yonkers from Albany, New York which was upstate. The two have been close ever since, but Styles normally worked a 9 to 5 at Wal-Mart until he recently lost his job. To only make matters worse, his girl was expecting a daughter any day now. So, coming out here with Black was his only option.

Black was Wolf's older brother. At the age of twenty-five, he robbed over twenty banks with success all over the East Coast. He was tall, skinny, dark skin, bug eyes, short hair, big ears. He wasn't too handsome, but he could get by because he had swag. Black looks nothing like his brothers CB or Wolf, but he and CB had the same dad along with their deceased sister. When Rita told him about Victoria being killed recently, he was hurt because she had a bright career. Even though he was never around, he still loved his sister and brother. Black lived in the Bronx with his girlfriend Katrina who was a scammer, but now she took care of their two-year-old son, Joshua Jr.

Robbing banks was his profession, he took great pride in his craft. He always scopes out a bank for a couple of days before he made his move. Normally, he would go on his missions alone because he didn't have time to babysit or worry about a nigga snitching on him.

"Stick to the plan and let me handle the money. you post up at the door near the guards. if any of them move, bust their ass," Black said, passing him a loaded Draco and a mask.

"I got it, bro," Styles said, placing his mask over his face. Both men saw that the block was empty, and no civilians were outside, so they hopped out the Jeep and began creeping across the street in the early morning.

"Everybody get the fuck down!" Black yelled, kicking one of the fat security guards on the floor. Everybody slowly got on the floor, screaming. There were only nine civilians waiting in line and three bank tellers behind the counter.

Styles aimed his Draco at both of the guards while looking around making sure nobody was on their phone or doing no funny busy.

Black jumped over the counter in a swift jump, pointing his Draco at three older white women.

"Where is it at? And make sure there are no dye bombs, or I swear I'll kill you bitches!" Black shouted.

One of the women pointed at a small, open safe next to a bag.

"Back up and put your hands in the air now," Black yelled, opening the safe to see stacks of blue faces. He placed all the money in the bag while keeping his eyes on the women who looked spooked.

Once all the money was in the bag, Black jumped over the counter and ran out of the bank with Styles behind him. Before they even made it into the middle of the street, shots weaved past them. Black turned around to see Styles caught a headshot and was on the pavement leaking out the back of his head. Black let off his weapon, hitting one of the guards in his stomach twice and taking chunks out his liver and kidney.

The other guard took cover behind a mailbox giving Black enough time to make it to his Jeep burning rubber down the street. Before the police could arrive, Black was already on the interstate.

When Black was far away from the crime scene, his heart rate slowed down. He couldn't believe Styles was gone so fast. He told him to watch their back on the come out because the guards always tried to pursue the robbers.

Black smiled to himself, looking at the money on the passenger floor because he didn't have to share it with anyone.

****

Auburn Maximum-Security Prison

"Push, push, push!" OG yelled to CB who was bench pressing two-hundred and twenty-five pounds for the twenty-fifth time.

CB struggled on his last rep, but he was able to hang the weight back on the rack as OG spotted him in the weights shack outside in the prison yard.

"Good job today, but it seems like something is on your mind," OG said to CB who stood up and picked up the towel to wipe his sweat.

"My little sister was killed. She was about to go to college on a full ride scholarship for basketball," CB said, sadly as OG's face frowned with a hurtful look of pain in his eyes.

"I'm sorry… I can only imagine how you feel. That shit just hit me hard, CB, but be strong. You know we can't show no type of emotion in the belly of the beast," OG said, seriously, in his Brooklyn accent.

"I know," CB said, seeing inmates going back to their blocks through the yard. A group of Bloods shouted CB out on his way back to D-Block.

CB was serving a ten to life bid up north for a first-degree murder he caught seven years ago in Yonkers on Elm Street. A nigga tried to rob him, and CB killed him with three shots to the chest when he was twenty years old on his birthday.

He was high yellow complexion, tall, long braids, Spanish features, handsome, brown hazel eyes, and very stocky weighing two-hundred and thirty-five pounds solid.

Since he'd been locked up, he became a Blood gang member under a Brim set and he quickly rose to a high rank because he put in a lot of work behind the wall while he was in Attica.

OG was his neighbor from Brooklyn. He'd been down for over seventeen years, serving four life sentences for murders and drugs. He schooled CB on life, prison, morals, and he helped him gain a GED and a college degree in Business Management.

CB and OG went to their cells with the thick bars and cocked a seafood rice meal with Tyson chicken on their crockpots to feed their muscles.

Chapter 5

Yonkers, NY

Today was Victoria's funeral and the Protestant church was crowded with teenagers, friends, and family of Victoria.

Wolf and Rita sat in the front listening to Victoria's friends give speeches, saying their goodbyes, and crying their hearts out over their loss.

Rita held Wolf's hand in tears, trying her best not to scream, yell, or breakdown. The past two weeks had been rough for her; she had to take off from work just to get herself together.

She knew many mothers who lost their child due to violence or stray bullets, but never would she think she would witness it firsthand.

The same day Victoria was killed, she got a scholarship to her dream school. Howard University.

It was time for Rita and Wolf to get their last look at Victoria before they buried her across town. Rita stood up, looked around the bright church to see everybody grieving in tears which made her realize what type of affect her beautiful daughter had on others.

Wolf walked his mom up the stairs and when she saw Victoria laying stiff in her casket in a white dress with her arms crossed looking like a beautiful angel, it made her realize she was never going to see her baby again.

"Noooo, baby! Why you? Why Lord? Why my baby?" Rita cried, leaning into Victoria's casket hugging her.

Wolf let his mom mourn because he knew how important it was. He felt the same way his mom did, but he knew that he had to be strong not only for himself but his mom also.

When everything was over, Wolf was walking with Rita outside into the heat to see Black walking towards them.

"Where is she?" Black asked his mom, who looked at him like he had four heads before she slapped the fuck out of him. The smack was so loud people in the parking lot directed their attention to them.

"How dare you disrespect your sister by not even coming to her funeral? She was your blood! How self-centered and ignorant can you fucking be?" she asked him with tears rolling down her cheeks.

"I'm sorry, mom. It was just hard to look at her like this," Black said.

"That's the best you can come up with you should be ashamed of yourself as a man and a brother fucking clown," Rita said, walking off pissed.

"Just give her some time, bro. You know how she is," Wolf told his brother.

"I already know. But nobody knows who killed her?" Black asked.

"Nah, you know how Yonkers PD is. If it's not a white person getting slumped, then they don't care," Wolf said seriously watching him mom climb in his BMW

"Facts. You good? How's school?"

"I'm okay and school is good. I just had to take a couple of weeks off because of this, but I graduate soon," he said.

"Good. I'm proud of you, bro. I know you don't see me anymore, but I'm raising a child and living my life. You know what I'm into, so I stay away and keep a distance for everybody's safety," Black said.

"I feel you, bro. I ain't trippin'. I know how it goes, but it's good to see you. I'ma take mommy home," Wolf said about walking off.

"Before you go," Black said, pulling out a wad of money handing it to Wolf.

"Bro, I'm good."

"No, take it. Bro, I'll see you around," Black said, walking away from the church.

Wolf placed the money in his pocket before walking to his car to take Rita home.

This was the first time he saw Black in months. He knew his brother was a bank robber, shit the whole Yonkers did.

Inside the car, Rita stared at him oddly as he pulled off away from the church lot.

"Why did you take his money? Black is all for self, he doesn't understand the value of family and you can never trust a man with those types of morals. I raised you better than any of my children, so I expect better from you now and as you grow into a man," she said.

"I know, mom."

"Good. Let's go to the waterfront. It's a nice day. Why don't you have a girlfriend? You're very handsome and educated. I saw all them girls on your social media. Please don't tell me your gay?" she asked with a straight face.

"Mom… Hell no, I'm not gay. I'm just waiting on the right one to be real," he chuckled.

"Good smart because these girls out here nowadays are thots as you kids say," she said, making him laugh.

"You're right, but I do have someone in mind. I'm feeling a Puerto Rican chick that I go to college with," he said, stopping on a hill at a red light.

"Ummm, okay. Good. Take your time," she said. They went to the river and tried to get Victoria off their mind.

****

Champ and Fred just pulled away from the church parking lot where Victoria's funeral was held today.

"The whole city came out to show ole girl love must have been someone special," Fred said in the passenger seat of the Benz 600.

"She was a basketball star. Nigga, did you see the news?" Champ asked.

"I don't watch the news, bro. I'm too busy for that shit. But you saw that cat, Black?"

"Yeah. What about him, bro?"

"He must be related to the chick. Ain't he a big-time bank robber?"

"Yeah, but son not a killer, so we good. The other nigga who we shot look like a schoolboy, so our only problem is Andy and we need to find him because he had to know it was us," Champ said, driving through his hood full of Crips.

"He killed my brother. I can't wait to pull up on him," Fred said.

"Soon," Champ said, sounding positive they will find Andy, who was a known gunslinger and stick up kid.

Chapter 6

NYU college
One Week Later

Wolf was in the student hall, studying for his big exams in two days and he was waiting on Bella to bring him the recent notes she took, so he could copy them. Missing school because of his sister's death took a small toll on him because he loved his school. He was a full-time student.

It was his first day back at school and his first class was in less than an hour, but he needed Bella to hurry up with her notes so he could catch up. Both of them had two classes together, so that was a blessing for him. If he didn't know something, she knew it. With a 4.6 GPA, she was very smart and witty, that's what Wolf liked about her. She was a beauty, kind, and educated on everything.

He saw Bella rush into the student hall downstairs and he waved her upstairs.

"Romeo," she said, hugging him tightly.

"Somebody missed me," he said, inhaling her Gucci perfume.

"I heard what happened to your sister and you on the news. I'm so sorry."

"It's okay. Thank you," he said, seeing she had on a police uniform. "Why you dressed like a cop?" he asked.

"I started the police academy today. I passed my tests with flying colors, so your girl is about to be Yonkers' finest," she said, flexing her arms.

"Yonkers... Don't you live in Peekskill?"

"Yeah, but they sending me to Yonkers because they need more officers out there since it's too much crime."

"I live there. I know," he replied.

"Anyway, here is everything you need, and don't lose my shit like last time," she said, handing him a pink notebook full of notes.

"Damn," Wolf said, trying to understand her fancy handwriting.

"Beggars can't be picky, but I have to go, handsome. See you later," she said, getting up to head out.

"Aye?"

"B," she said, turning around.

"Thanks."

"Anytime, big head. You better ace it," she said, looking at him one more time before walking down the stairs.

Wolf was happy for her. This was all she talked about since a freshman and now she was starting the academy. She deserved it.

***

Bella, whose real name was Isabella Aguilera, got off at the Yonkers exit and listened to her GPS navigate her through the dangerous streets of Yonkers.

This was her sixth time to Yonkers, out of her twenty-one years on earth. Her father, who was an FBI agent, didn't like her going to dangerous areas like Yonkers, Mount Vernon, or the Bronx which was all within walking distance.

Bella was eye candy everywhere she went. The males couldn't keep their eyes off of her. She was white and Puerto-Rican. Her mom was a white woman that died of cancer years ago. Her father, Richard Aguilera, was Puerto Rican and a dirty FBI Agent.

Most people thought she was white because of her complexion and bright, greenish eyes that matched Wolf's. She was short, small waist, nice round ass, long and curly dark brown hair, with a pair of nice, firm titties.

She found the big building that looked like the DMV and parked next to a SWAT truck. She got out a little nervous while the blazing heat had heat waves everywhere.

"Excuse, me. I'm Ms. Aguilera, here to begin my training," Bella told an old white lady sitting at the lobby desk in a white shirt, sizing her up. The older woman grabbed a clipboard looking for her name.

"Okay, you're right. Ms. Aguilera, I believe your squad is about to start their training in twenty minutes. Your exercise gear is downstairs in locker twenty-two which will be your assigned locker," she said, giving her a small lock for the locker.

"Thanks, Ms. Taylor," she replied, looking at her name on her shirt.

"You seem like a sweet and beautiful girl. Word of advice. Put on our poker face or they will run all over you. The criminals and your so-called fellow officers. I don't know what you saw on TV, but all that serve and protect shit is a fallacy. It's a dog eat dog world. I've been on the force twenty-six years, trust me. Now, go show them what you got," she said, walking off.

Bella turned to leave with a different facial expression. She walked past cops eyeing her with lust in their eyes making her feel uncomfortable.

Once the locker room was empty, she hurried up to dress into a YPD sweatsuit and made her way out back.

"Listen up, I'm Sergeant Andrew Scott and I will be training you maggots for the next six weeks. My goal is to break you and send you home crying to your family until you realize that being a cop isn't for you. The weak will not make it. I'm sorry, not here in Yonkers. We have the most murders, drug cases, police killings, civilian killings, assaults, rapes, and kidnapping in Westchester County. You will see a lot of shit that may traumatize you. You may have to kill a thug. You may have to be a dirty cop at times. Can you all handle that?" Sergeant Scott said, walking back and forth. He was looking at the twenty-six soon to be officers.

"Half of you won't make it out of the academy, to be honest, but you could always work for FedEx or UPS. They're always hiring," Sergeant Scott stated with a serious face. "Today, you will run ten miles in a reasonable amount of time, even you, cupcake," Sergeant Scott said to a chunky Black chick.

Bella stood in line listening and thinking what the fuck did she get herself into. She wasn't going to give up or let Sergeant Scott break her.

There was a small track in the back and a small obstacle course set up for training. Before half of the day was over, three niggas passed out in the heat and left on stretchers. Sergeant Scott explained that if one couldn't make it through the obstacle course, then they weren't physically fit to be a cop, so they failed

Romell Tukes

Chapter 7

Yonkers, NY

"Yo, Andy! Where the fuck you get all this shit?" Lil Tom said, sitting in his room with four of his friends bagging up pounds of Kush into ounces and quarters.

Lil Tom was Andy's little nigga who lived on Elm Street, a couple of buildings down from his crib.

"Yeah son, this loud some gas," one of the youngins said, coughing off the smoke he was inhaling.

"Just know it's a lot more of where that came from. All y'all little niggas go to high school, so selling this shit should be easy. Everybody profit is 50/50," Andy said, moving a loaded .9mm sitting on a computer chair to sit down.

Lil Tom was known for keeping guns because his older brother was in the marines and he stole weapons from the base. He would come back to Yonkers to sell them with Lil Tom's help.

"Any of y'all niggas see Champ lately?" Andy asked, knowing his young boys were in the field.

"Nah, son be on Riverdale. Niggas don't fuck with that wild nigga over here," JC said.

"Didn't he kill your brother last summer, bro?" Lil Tom asked, opening a pound of Kush and weighing it on a scale.

"Yeah, I'ma get that nigga soon," JC said.

"I heard he killed Vicky who lives up the block. That's fucked up and she was bad," Lil Tom added.

"Word, son. That was him," Cut said, pausing the XBOX game.

"Yeah, that's what the streets talking about, but that nigga body count is up there," Lil Tom said.

"Well look, if any of you see this nigga, take his head off and I'ma look out," Andy said.

"Say less. We on it, boy. But what's good with Smurf? I heard he touch soon," JC said.

"Yeah, he in Five Point with Moreno, but he good. His wifey about to pull up on him and I gotta get his package ready. I gotta go.

Yo JC, let me holla at you outside. You heard," Andy said, getting up to leave because he had something important to take care of tonight.

Outside it was dark on the one-way block as both men posted up on the stairs.

"What's up, Andy?"

"What's popping with Cut? I heard he got booked with a gun in White Plains two days ago. How he get out that fast?"

"He said his mom bailed him out," JC said, wondering the same thing.

"How he make bail on a weekend without seeing a judge and on probation? Bro, watch that nigga. Son, sumthin ain't right," Andy said, unaware of the GMC truck creeping up the one-way.

"Boy been acting real funny too. Asking a lot of questions about bodies from last summer when we was warring with the GMG niggas."

"That nigga might be a dubb..." Andy said.

Bloc! Bloc! Bloc! Bloc!

Shots rang out from the GMC truck. Andy pulled out his Glock, shooting back at the truck while it raced off down the thin dark street.

"Help..." JC said, holding his bloody chest from being shot four times. Lil Tom and his crew ran downstairs with Draco's and AK's to see JC breathing hard. Andy got off the block, he knew the police would arrest him.

Civilians called the police, while JC's friends tried to put pressure on the bullet wounds, but it wasn't working. JC died seconds before the police arrived. He was only sixteen years old.

***

Brooklyn, NY

Shantell was dancing in Club Lust tonight. She wore a one-piece, G-string bikini covering her nipples and pussy, but her pussy lips still poked out. She worked the floor tonight, dancing on ballers and thirsty niggas. She was too tired to work the stage and her feet hurt. The strip club was litty tonight. Two up and coming rappers from Brooklyn were in the building blowing bands on the dancers. There was a nigga upstairs in the private VIP area by himself popping bottles and dripping in ice with four chains, two bust down Rolexes, and a diamond grill in his mouth.

Shantell could tell he wasn't that cute, but money could make any ugly nigga look like Denzel Washington. She made her way upstairs with her sexy and sassy walk.

"What's up, Papi? You want some company?"

"Yeah, come in ma," he said, looking at her body and feeling his dick get harder. Shantell sat right on his lap, wiggling her big ass on his erection.

"What's your name?" Mozzy said, smelling her sweet perfume.

"Whatever you want it me to be, Papi."

"I'ma call you bands, ma, but I'm trying to get a piece of this," he said, sliding a finger into her wet pussy as she moaned.

"I need two stacks, pop," she said, turning around and facing him.

"I got five for you, ma. We can slide back to my hotel across town," Mozzy said, pulling out a wad of blue faces with a rubber band and handing it to her.

"Damn, okay. We out, but first, let me give you a little taste," she said, undoing his Fendi belt and pulling out his nice size dick, then sliding it into her pussy.

Shantell rode his dick slowly grinding on his lap while he gripped her waist, guiding her up and down.

"Uhmmm shittt…" he screamed, spreading her tight strong walls open.

"Yessss. Hit that shit, Papi," she cried, bouncing up and down on his dick. Mozzy sucked on her titties trying to control himself from cumming, but her pussy was so good. He couldn't hold back.

"I'm cumminggg," he said, making her hop off and jerk his dick while spitting on it.

Shantell didn't suck dick, kiss niggas, or do anal. She only did those sexual fantasies with her man, Smurf.

When he came, she caught it with a napkin and cleaned his dick, looking at all the wetness around his thigh area on his Balenciaga jeans.

"What's up with some head, ma? Your pussy is grade A. I'm trying to see what that mouth do," Mozzy said standing up ready to finish the party at his hotel.

"Let's save that for round two," she said, picking up her money on her way downstairs to get dressed and leave.

***

Downtown Brooklyn, NY

Mozzy and Shantell entered the hotel room, both horny and ready to finish where they left off.

"Let me freshen up then we can get to it."

"Fuck that! I'm trying to eat that thing just like that!"

"Ewww Papi, you nasty. Just give me a second. Relax, you got me all night. I'm all yours," she said walking into the bathroom. Mozzy quickly stripped down and started Crip walking naked around the hotel room.

Mozzy was a Crip nigga from Brooklyn in the Flatbush area. He was a heroin plug and was getting to a bag. When he heard the bathroom water shut off, he sat on the bed stroking his dick back to life.

Shantell came out of the bathroom fully dressed

"I left my outfit in the car. I'ma go get it," she said, walking out the room.

"Damn bitch," he whispered to himself. When the door opened again, he was lying down, legs cocked open.

"Where your shit at nigga?" Andy rushed into the room scaring the shit out of Mozzy. When Mozzy jumped up, Andy started to pistol-whip him until he folded in a fetal position crying like a bitch. He fucked around and shitted on himself. There were shit tards dropping everywhere.

Shantell ran back into the room taking Mozzy's jewelry, clothes, socks, wallet, everything he had on his body.

"Now, let's try this again. I know a baller like yourself don't leave the house empty-handed," Andy said, screwing a silencer on his Glock 17.

"It's in the trunk, man," Mozzy said, unable to see out his busted left eye from the gruesome pistol-whipping. Andy looked at Shantell who went outside to check the trunk.

"You let a bitch get you. Nigga you're a dumb ass nigga. It was too easy. You know these New York bitches be on grimy time," Andy said, feeling sorry for him a little. Shantell came back inside with a Louis Vuitton bookbag full of money.

"You ready?" she asked Andy before he shot Mozzy eight times, reconstructing his face. Andy and Shantell left, sharing everything 50/50. They headed back to Yonkers, laughing, and joking about Mozzy.

Romell Tukes

Chapter 8

Upstate, NY

Shantell had been on the road in her red Lexus RX Coupe since four in the morning. She was on her way to visit Smurf in Five Point Correctional Facility. She made sure that she came to visit him twice a month. Wherever he was, she was coming.

Last night was crazy. She didn't want to fuck Mozzy in the club, but she had to hook him in, so he would fall into her trap. She called it the pussy trap.

She always called Andy when she saw a real potential come up, but she never saw Andy kill a nigga until last night. Seeing Mozzy get murdered replayed in her mind ever since seeing his face split open with hot bullets.

Growing up in Yonkers, she was used to violence, but seeing it up close and hearing about it was two different things. She heard lots of stories about Andy and Smurf, how they killed a lot of niggas in the town, but she never questioned Smurf or asked him because she played her role.

Life was rough for her as a kid growing up in the School Street projects in the same building that DMX was from. Her mother is a crackhead, her brother is a Latin King doing sixty to life at the state prison called Sing Sing. She sent him money, pics, and food monthly.

Chasing a bag was all she knew, so dancing was her blessing. She also went to Westchester Community College four days a week taking Accountant classes.

At the gate, the guards checked her I.D. before letting her into the prison which is in the middle of nowhere. All anyone could see was fences, woods, and deer everywhere.

Shantell made sure she wore appropriate attire, or they would reject her visit. She saw so many families drive eight to ten hours to see their loved ones to only be turned around because their clothes were too tight.

She grabbed Smurf thirty-five-pound bag of food and some *Buttman, Thick, and GYRO magazines* that Andy put together for him. Andy also placed six compressed ounces of exotic weed in a peanut butter jar for him as he did for his boy every month.

Inside, Shantell had to clear the metal detectors, then bring the food and magazines to the package room so the prison guards could check the items. They would then give it to the inmates after their visits.

Almost after an hour of waiting, she was brought out to the 'dance floor' as inmates called it. The visiting room was half full today, but it was still early. After six hours of driving, she was tired. She only got three hours of sleep, but she had to come to see her boo.

Thirty minutes later, Smurf walked out the back with a pair of red Gucci shoes, collared shirt, green state-issued pants, and Cartier glasses.

"What's popping, beautiful?" Smurf said, kissing her thick juicy lips.

"Hey," she said, blushing. She was so happy to see him.

"You look tired, love. How was your ride?"

"I'm drained, but the ride was regular. I had a crazy night. I met this nigga at a club, fucked him for two seconds, then went back to the hotel. I had Andy there, but I never saw him, you know…" she said, giving him the crazy eyes and making him laugh because he knew Andy was a hitter just like him.

"That's a part of the game, you heard. But just don't think about it. How much?"

"Seventy-thousand a piece. Both of us put ten thousand dollars in your account and that shit is looking nice for when you touch. I believe you have about fifty- thousand dollars in there," she said, trying to remember.

"Good. That's love. I'm not trying to come home fucked up. My little mans from the Bronx went home fucked up and robbed two niggas, killing both of them to only catch a life bid in the Feds with some Makk Ballers," Smurf said, sadly, shaking his head.

"I don't need that to happen to you. But do you know I saw your old side bitch two weeks ago in the club with your cousin balling?" she said, rolling her eyes because she hated to bring up her name.

Smurf cheated on Shantell with a bad Puerto Rican bitch from Yonkers, but when he got locked up, the Puerto Rican bitch and his own cousin stole his guns and $150,000 from his crib in Glenwood.

Andy wanted to kill his bitch and cousin, but Smurf told him nah, even though half of the money was Andy's.

"Don't worry about them, love. I will handle them when the time comes. But how's college?"

"Good, I be so busy with work and school. I have no time for me, daddy. I can't wait for you to come home to put that good dick down on a bitch."

"I bet."

"I sent the two money orders to your friends. They should have it this week."

"Good. My celly is fucked up in here. He got a lot of time and my old head doing a stretch alone also, so I just like to make sure niggas I fuck with is good."

"That's why I love you, Papi. You got a good evil heart," she said, laughing. They spent the rest of the visit catching up.

***

Greenburg, NY

"It's three inside, keeps your eyes open," Agent Aguilera told his partner, Agent Scott. The two FBI agents posted on the wall in the back of a blue house which was a kingpin's stash house in a middle-class neighborhood.

BOOM!

"Freeze FBI!" Agent Aguilera screamed with his gun drawn. One of the criminals tried to run.

Bloc! Bloc! Bloc! Bloc!

Agent Aguilera shot him in the back, killing the young black man.

"Where is your boss?" Agent Scott asked the two young black males that were sitting at a table full of bricks of coke and money.

"You just killed him."

"Oops, did I do that? Where's the rest of the drugs at?" Agent Aguilera said, placing his gun to the dark, fat drug dealer.

"Are you muthafuckers even cops? Everything is under the sink and right there," the fat one said.

Bloc! Bloc! Bloc! Bloc!

Agent Aguilera killed him, and Agent Scott followed his lead, shooting the other hustler in his head.

"Bag this shit up then we call it in," Agent Aguilera said looking under the sink to see three duffle bags of drugs inside.

Agent Aguilera was Bella's father. He was an FBI agent in Westchester County and for the Bronx. He was a dirty cop with a long resume of harassing civilians, assaults and tampering with evidence. He'd been an agent for twenty-two years.

He was 100% Puerto Rican born in Puerto Rico but raised in the Bronx. He was tall, handsome for a man in his early forties, and a five o'clock shadow on his face. He was married to a beautiful white woman named Ann. But when she died, his life changed forever. He was forced to raise a daughter by himself.

After losing his wife, he moved to Peekskill with his daughter and he became a corrupt agent, having no pity or mercy for no soul.

Agent Scott, his partner, was a young black man with five years on his resume following Aguilera moves to get some extra cash to feed his family.

Chapter 9

Yonkers, NY

Officer Sanderson and Officer Steels were with Yonkers police department and two of the worst cops in Westchester county. Everybody called the two white racist men Beavis and Butthead from the early 90's tv show.

The two partners robbed drug dealers, planted drugs and guns on niggas, beat niggas up, and harassed anybody with an unknown name who wasn't paying street taxes.

What they were most famous for was picking up criminals and gangsters at nighttime, beating them up, then dropping them off in a hood they had beef with. Two niggas recently died going into the wrong hood thanks to Beavis and Butthead.

They sat in their black Dodge Challenger with tints eating dinner in a shopping center parking lot on a small break. It was 6 pm and there were no calls, so it was their chill time.

"I heard the FEDs did a sweep in Peekskill again this morning," Officer Steels said, taking a bite out of a deli sandwich.

"I bet that shit had Agent Aguilera's name all over it. I hate that dick sucker," Sanderson stated.

"He's alright, but it's a lot of money up there in Peekskill. We should take a trip out there one of these days because it seems like these streets are getting dry like your wife's pussy," Steels said, laughing.

"At least I got one. I can only imagine how many STD's you caught fucking with them nightwalkers on Nepperhan Avenue," Sanderson shot back.

"I only got burnt three times. I use protection now. Why you always gotta throw that shit in my face?" Steels said, seriously. He sat watching a Black kid in a gray hoodie walk through the lot with a backpack on and walking fast.

"You see this little nigga?" Sanderson said, looking out the window.

"Yeah let's go. It could be our lucky day," Steels said, rushing out of the car to catch up with the kid.

"Aye you, stop!" Sanderson yelled as the kid continued to speed walk. "Stop you, little bastard!" Sanderson yelled, grabbing him by his hoodie.

When the Black kid turned around nervously, he reached in his hoodie packet to pause his iPod because he had his headphones on full blast.

"He got a gun!" Steels yelled, shooting him five times and then Sanders also shot the kid twice for good measures.

Boc! Boc! Boc! Boc! Boc!

The bullets entered the kid's heart, killing him instantly. When they saw his face, he looked retarded or if he had some type of special disease.

"Call it in," Sanderson said, checking the kid's pockets for any weapons they could use in their defense. Sanderson saw the kid was only 15 years old with mental health disorders and medical issues.

"I called it in. Here, put this pocket knife on him and put his prints on it," Steels said as his partner did as his partner said, knowing they fucked up again.

***

Elmsford, NY

Sanderson spent five hours doing a ton of paperwork for the killing of the young African-American male who was labeled as retarded.

Steels did overtime and Sanderson just arrived at his home at midnight. He told his wife he was doing overtime, but he was drained from the long day.

Sanderson told his boss the retarded kid tried to attack him with a pocketknife and his boss went for it because he knew anything was capable to happen in Yonkers.

At forty, Sanderson lived a regular life off-duty. He had a beautiful wife, Megan, no kids, a nice apartment, two cars, and a fair marriage. Lately, their sex life had been below regular, but he was going to make that up tonight.

He walked into his home to see the lights on in the living room and kitchen. He had a feeling his wife was asleep, so he crept through the apartment which was clean, large, polish with new carpets and furniture. Sanderson went towards the master bedroom to see the light was on from under the door. When he opened the door, he was shocked and stuck when he saw Megan on her knees sucking a big Black guy's dick, making love to it.

"Megan!" Sanderson yelled, snapping her out of her sexual pleasure.

"Baby!" she said, jumping up and tossing her robe over her body. The stocky Black guy quickly got dressed in an army uniform. He was their neighbor.

"Megan, what the fuck are you doing? You're fucking our neighbor!" he shouted, mad he left his gun in the car.

"Baby, I'm sorry, but I want to be with James," Megan said.

"It's Jamell," he said, correcting her.

"What about our marriage?"

"I'm sorry, but I can't do this anymore. I'm not happy. I made a mistake marrying you. I'm a lawyer and you're a cop. I need excitement and I get all of that from James," Megan stated, seriously.

"It's Jamell. What the fuck?" he said again.

"Sorry daddy," she said, rubbing his muscular chest.

"Okay fine. I am going to file for divorce, but get the fuck out of my house."

"This is my house, your name is not on the lease, love. I'm sorry," Megan said with a smirk.

"Fuck you, bitch!" Sanderson said, walking out sick. *I can't believe I just lost my wife to a nigger,* he thought.

***

Yonkers, NY

There was a night basketball game on Warburton Avenue at the park and half the city came out to see the best basketball players in the city turn up.

Jadakiss and Styles P came out to show support to their hometown. Big man was on the game tonight and Champ was there with his crew on the sideline cheering for his team.

Champ came to every basketball game, he loved how litty the games were. He was strapped and ready to smoke a nigga if anybody jumped out there.

"Damn it!" he shouted, seeing his team was fouling out in the last quarter.

When the game was over, the crowd left the court before someone got killed or shot like last week.

Champ was leaving with three of his goons when he saw his ex-girlfriend, Erica, with a couple of her homegirls all looking like a snack.

Erica was Andy's wifey and she was the person he needed to see.

"Erica, what's up? Bitch, where is your man at?" Champ asked her, standing in her face.

"What nigga? Boy, please. Nobody got time for you. Leave my man alone. Don't be mad because Andy got the best pussy you ever had bum nigga," she said as her girls laughed.

Champ slapped Erica so hard in her face, her head bounced off her friend's shoulder. Champ walked off laughing and left her crying while her friend comforted her.

Chapter 10

White Plains, NY

Andy pulled up to Erica's job at the White Plains Clinic, where she worked for two years. He just copped a new, pearl-white Audi A7. It was clean with black leather, a digital dashboard, tints with curtains in the windows, and heated seats for the cold New York winters.

Since he'd been stacking a lot of money, he wanted to take Erica on a shopping spree and out to dinner in the city somewhere special.

Erica was his rock. She was a down ass bitch with no cuts or in between. She always got to her own bag, so she wouldn't have to ask her man or no nigga for nothing.

The weed, pills, and molly he had moving in his hood was doing good, but Andy needed a plug on some bricks because crack on Elm Street was like the new '80s.

He saw Erica come out looking for his Benz, but she didn't see it. He switched his cars more than she switched her work uniform.

Beep, beep.

Andy rolled down the windows so she could see him.

"Damn boy, who you stole this from?" she said, kissing his lips.

"You got jokes, but this is yours," he said, pulling off while Summer Walker played low on the stereo.

"Oh my God! Baby, for real?" she screamed.

"I know you wanted a white Audi and you deserve it, babe. So, you can turn in your Range. This shit paid for already," he said.

"You're the best. Let's go home so I can fuck the shit outta you," she said.

"We going to get to that, but first, we going to White Plains Mall to do some shopping, and then we're going to the city for dinner," he said.

"Nigga, it's not Valentine's Day or my birthday. Who you got pregnant?" she said, seriously ready to punch him dead in his face.

"I can't treat my lady sometimes?"

"Hell no, nigga," she said, looking out the windows about to pull into the mall garage.

"Well today, I am. I haven't seen you in two days."

"Yeah, you haven't been home. I wonder why," she said, sucking her teeth. She was feeling like he'd been up to no good.

"I was at Mooky's crib. You know how my cousin is, babe. But how was the game yesterday?"

"I've been meaning to tell you something, but I don't want you to get mad," she said.

"What's up?" Andy replied, parking.

"Please don't get mad, but I was chilling with Ma, Lala, and Raven enjoying ourselves. My ex-boyfriend, Champ, walks up to me asking me questions about you," she said, pausing.

"And what? Fuck that nigga," he added.

"We went back and forth, then he slapped me in front of everybody. I didn't even know what to do," she said. Andy's anger was rising.

"I'ma handle it."

"Baby, please don't do anything to him. He's not worth it."

"Erica, I don't want to talk about it no more. Let's enjoy the day," he said, climbing out of the car.

The first store they hit was the Louis Vuitton store. Erica went crazy picking out heels, dresses, purses, and scarves. Andy let her get whatever she wanted it was her day, but he couldn't get Champ off his mind.

There was no doubt he was going to make him pay for what he did to his wifey.

Erica was black and white, very light skin, sparkling hazel eyes, short and thick with 36-29-51 measurements. She rocked her short hair, with cute dimples in her rosy cheeks. She was a little older than Andy at twenty-eight, but her life was in the right direction. She loved the hell outta Andy like no other man.

***

Auburn Maximum Prison

"I'll see you when you get back from dancing with the star, have a good one," OG Chuck yelled to CB when he saw him walk past his cell for a visit.

"Good looks, OG!"

"You already know, hot boy. See you when you get back, Blood," his homie, Two Guns, said when CB walked up to his cell bars.

"I thought you were coming down for a visit too?" CB asked his homie who got visits every weekend from his baby mother who was a sexy Haitian bitch.

"Nah, shawty went to DR to get her ass done," Two Guns said.

"A'ight skrap, I'ma 212 with you when I get back Eastside," CB said before walking off.

CB wore a tight white V-neck shirt flexing his big muscles and lean body. A couple of the visitors did a quick glance, liking what they saw. CB saw his visitor seated near the snack machine as always.

"CB," Britt said, getting up to hug him and passionately kiss him.

CB sat down swallowing four loonies full of heroin and weed. Britt was his mule, she traveled eight hours to bring him drugs and she got paid two bands a trip, which was well worth it.

She was close to three hundred pounds, black, with big lips and teeth, but she was a sweetheart.

"What's going with you?" CB asked her.

"Working hard at Family Dollar trying to take care of my seven-year-old son," she said.

"That's what popping. Work hard and stay focused."

"Yeah, shit is so hard nowadays. You have no clue; everything is so fast. Coming up here helps me more than it may help you and your homies," she said, staring at the snack machine and looking at the newest Debbie cake.

"I feel you, ma," he said, seeing her attention was elsewhere. "Treat yourself, gurl," he said.

"Yeah, I've been on my walking and dieting shit. I lost twenty pounds already," she said.

"Where?" he said in a low pitch voice.

"Excuse me?"

"I said, yea, I see," CB replied, laughing in his mind. He sat watching her walk her fat ass to the snack machine and spend close to eighty dollars on herself and not even offering him anything.

Chapter 11

Yonkers, NY

Fred was waiting in a semi-full barbershop on Riverdale, waiting for his barber to get done with one of his clients. Since killing Victoria with Champ, he'd been out of sight trying to stay out the streets. Summer was almost over, so he figured it was cool to show his face again.

The police still never found his brother's body, but he thought about the scene of him burying his brother every night. He had no clue that Champ was so cold-hearted.

"Fred, you ready, baby boy?" his barber said, collecting money from one of his clients.

"Let's do it," Fred said, getting in the chair.

"Where you been at son? I ain't see you or your brother in weeks," the barber said.

"You know how it be," Fred replied while his barber started cutting his hair.

When he was done, Fred paid his barber of ten years and left. He parked his Cadillac OTS down the street behind an apartment building that he used to trap out of when he was heavy in the dope game before he had his kids.

It was getting cold outside and Fred had to go meet Champ in New Rochelle for whatever reason. Fred hopped in his car, but before he could close his door, someone slammed a brick into his face and knocked him clean out.

***

Wolf had been waiting for Fred to come out of the barbershop for an hour. He got the drop on him early this morning. On his way to school, he saw Fred talking to a nigga on Maple Street.

Instead of going to school, he followed the familiar face around all day, waiting for the perfect time to make his move.

Wolf grabbed Fred's keys, dragged his body out into the spacious trunk, and pulled off in the Cadillac.

Ten minutes later, Wolf parked in an abandoned factory near a Metro-North train station. Wolf climbed out with his .9mm handgun that Black gave him when he turned sixteen to protect himself.

When he popped the trunk, Fred tried to jump out and take off until Wolf slapped him with the butt of the gun.

"Aaahhhh!"

"Shut your bitch ass up and get the fuck out," Wolf said coldly as Fred did what he said in slow motion, knowing he meant business.

"Look, bro, you got the wrong nigga. I don't even know you," Fred said with blood leaking down his face and walking into the empty factory filled with all types of machines.

"Stop," Wolf said, seeing a big press machine and ropes hanging from the machine handle. "You remember that young girl you and your friend killed at that high school? Well, that was my sister and you shot me," Wolf said with a malicious look on his face.

"I'm sorry that wasn't me... I swear that was Champ's idea I had nothing to do with that please man" he cried with a rueful facial expression.

"Walk to that machine," Wolf said, snatching the thick rope off of the machine handle. "Lay down on the belt."

"What?" Fred was about to protest until Wolf kicked him, sending him flying onto the belt. When Fred was stationed on the belt, Wolf tied him down so tight that he was unable to breathe.

"Who is Champ and where can I find him?"

"I don't know. He moves around so much," Fred said. Wolf turned on the green button on the old rusty machine and brought it to life. A large flat metal slab was coming down on Fred's body.

"Okay, okay, okay, okay!" he yelled, making Wolf stop the machine.

"Talk."

"He normally hangs out on Riverdale and 288 with his crew. He also got a baby mother over there. She stays in building 175 and her name is Jhena."

"Okay perfect," Wolf said pushing the green button watching the machine compress Fred's body as he screamed like a bitch. The machine squashed his body with ease crushing his bones, face, body, and organs until he looked like a pancake.

Blood spilled all over the place. Wolf stopped the machine and pressed the release button to see Fred's body unrecognizable.

"Wow," Wolf said. He did not want to touch the body, but he had to because he wanted to bring Fred's body to Champ's doorstep.

Wolf grabbed a piece of the rope and dragged the body across the cement floor, leaving a trail of blood and organs.

He placed Fred's body in the backseat of the Cadillac and drove back to Riverdale to park the car on the corner where Champ hangs out to send a message.

**

Washington Heights, NY

Andy was on Dyckman in a big park, shooting dice with a gang of Spanish niggas. There was over $300,000 on the floor while four heavy hitters went back to back shooting dice, playing Cee-lo on the handball court's wall.

"How much you got? It's your bet, Papi," a young Dominican nigga shouted, shaking dice in his hand ready to roll because his hand was on fire today.

"I got $100,000," Andy said, tossing a look on the floor like it was ten dollars.

"Bet… Get them, girl," the Dominican nigga said, shooting the dice to only ace out and lose. It was now Andy's roll and if he hit a 4, 5, 6, he won all the money on the floor.

Everybody in the park was silent watching, but this was an everyday thing on Dyckman. Niggas lost and won millions. Rappers, basketball players, and kingpins came out daily to shoot dice or enjoy the beautiful Dominican women all over the city.

Andy rolled the dice, praying to a trap God because he was down to his last $100,000. He had a bad gambling habit.

When the dice landed on 4, 5, 6 everybody went crazy. Andy couldn't believe the $400,000 on the floor was his. When he picked up his money, Lil Tom helped him. Both men were strapped just in case a nigga had ill attentions because niggas got robbed at dice games every day.

Andy collected his money and walked out of the park with Lil Tom.

"That was crazy. Did you see them niggas faces, son?" Lil Tom said, climbing into the new Mercedes Benz that he just brought thanks to the weed and pill flow on Elm Street.

"Yoooo..." a Dominican cat yelled, walking towards Andy.

"What's goody?" Andy said turning around on alert because he knew how niggas in the heights got down.

"I've seen you down here a couple of times and you look like you know how to get a bag," the Dominican dude said with a crew behind him.

"Facts."

"I'm Flaco. Where you from bro?" the young Flaco said, looking at Lil Tom ice grill him. He was ready to take his head off with any funny movement.

"I'm from Yonkers. They call me AD."

"Okay Y.O., but I'ma a plug out here. I'm doing big things. Take my math and call me. Maybe we can get up if that's what you are into," Flaco stated.

"A'ight." Andy pulled out his iPhone, punching in the number that Flaco told him.

Chapter 12

NYU
Weeks later

The college graduation was held out on the college football field. Everybody received their diploma and was ready to start their careers.

Wolf was so proud of himself. He finished college with flying colors, but he didn't plan to become a lawyer just yet.

"Romeo, oh my God! We did it," Bella said, hugging him.

"Facts. I'm so proud of you," Wolf said, looking at her curves under her open gown and manicured toes. "Damn, you look beautiful," Wolf said, making her blush.

"You know a bitch had to outdo these rachet busted bitches," she said looking around.

"Who was you with earlier?" Wolf asked, walking towards the parking lot since the ceremony was over.

"My dad, cousins, and babysitter, my nana. She basically raised me. Who came out for you?"

"Nobody. My ma had to work a double today," Wolf said.

"I see. Are you busy tonight?" she asked fretfully.

"Nothing at all. Why you ask?"

"You want to go out to grab a bite to eat somewhere in the city? I know the perfect place," she said

"Are you asking me on a date, Isabella?"

"No, I mean yeah…" she replied in a confused tone.

"I would love to," he said.

"I'll text you the info I'ma run home to take a shower and get dressed"

"Cool and it took you four years to ask me out on a date?" he asked

"You never asked. Bye," she said walking to her new Benz G 550 truck.

Wolf had been waiting for this day for years. He was feeling Bella since he first laid eyes on her, but they shared a friendship and he didn't want to fuck that up. He fucked three bitches in his school, but none of them could fuck with Bella on her worst day.

***

Lower East Side, NY
Hours Later

Wolf parked outside of the River Cafe to see Bella get out her Benz truck glowing. When he saw her tight, black and white dress with her Jimmy Choo's on her feet showing her nicely shaped legs, he felt an erection.

Wolf looked clean in his Ralph Lauren suit and shoes.

"Hey, you," Bella said, kissing him on his cheeks. They were holding hands like they were a real couple.

"You know how to drive a nigga crazy," he said making her laugh.

"Sometimes. Now come on. I'm starving," she said, walking through the door he opened for her.

After ordering their food and a few drinks they were comfortable and having a great time.

"I can't believe you're a cop now. That's crazy."

"All these crazy-ass drills, tests, and physical training. Shoot, I better be," she said.

"You exercise every day anyway, so that should be the easy part," he added.

"Yeah, I guess so. Ten people ain't make the cut, but I think I'ma do good. Yonkers PD is different than I thought. It's like they don't give a damn about protecting the public. I became a cop to protect and serve for our country, not kill civilians or hurt others," she said honestly.

Bella had been seeing a lot of things in the police station that made her question if she got into the right field.

"Fuck them, Bella. You don't have to follow their lead. Do what you know is right, ma. You have bad cops and good cops; it's up to you which one you want to be. Police recently killed a special needs kid in Yonkers and a police officer recently saved a little kid's life in a burning building, so it's always two kinds."

"You're right … What's your plan now?" she said/ drinking a Long Island iced tea.

"To be real and keep it a hundred, I'ma just weigh my options until I make the decision. I'm not sure if I want to join a law firm as an intern or take some other route that'll lead to me eventually starting a firm of my own."

"Sounds good. What's better than having your own company?" she said.

The dinner lasted two and a half hours, but Bella asked him to come back to Peekskill with her so they could go to the riverfront in her hood.

***

Peekskill, NY

Wolf followed her all the way back to Peekskill, which was an hour's drive. When they got to the riverfront, Wolf parked his BMW and hopped in her Benz truck looking over the riverfront.

"This is nice. I never really been out here. My bro, Bama, lives out here."

"I think I heard of him," she replied, staring into the stars.

"I was feeling you too. Now that we're here and both are single, why let our feelings go to waste?" she said leaning for a kiss. Wolf kissed her soft, perfect lips giving her a little tongue.

Bella let him suck on her neck, which was her hot spot, making her hot. Unable to control herself, she jumped in his lap feeling his dick pressed against her throbbing pussy.

"What are you doing?" Wolf asked, watching her pull out a condom from her purse and undo his belt buckle.

"Shhhh… I want to feel you inside of me, Papi," she said, pulling his dick out. She was impressed by his size while putting the golden condom on him.

Bella wore no panties, so she slid his tip into her gushy tight hole.

"Uhmmm…" she moaned, pressing her body forward as her hips slowly grind on him. Wolf was in the state of lust gripping her thin waist spreading her pussy walls open making her go crazy.

"Uggghhh fuckkk," she groaned while moving her hips faster and picking up her pace. She was feeling him deep in her guts.

Bella rode his dick with her arms wrapped around his neck. He brought her up and down on his dick until she reached her orgasm. Her pussy tightened and her body began to shake while her pussy contracted on his dick.

"Ahh, yesss! Sss! I'm about to cum…" she screamed, climaxing again in less than five seconds.

Wolf laid his seat all the way back and turned her around with his dick still in her. Bella rode his dick from the back holding on to the dashboard for safety while she bounced up and down on his dick.

The windows were tinted but fogged up. They fucked for forty-five minutes until they parted ways.

Neither one of them ever fucked outside, so it was a moment to remember.

Chapter 13

Dover, Delaware

Black walked into the Chase Bank in a suit and tie looking like a businessman trying to deposit a large amount of money. He waited in line behind the ropes, watching the bank tellers work in their station behind the fiberglass windows, which was bulletproof. This was his third time in the bank in the last week. He'd been staking it out for two weeks learning the ins and outs.

He knew that Chase Bank was one of the hardest banks to rob because they were all well secured. Black wore fake dreads, makeup to make his facial skin seem lighter, and colorful eye contacts.

There were two more civilians in front of him waiting in line. Black saw one security guard talking to a female, flirting and trying to bag her.

Black was now up. He walked to a fat black chick's window. She was smiling at him, looking him up and down.

"Good morning," the bank teller said, fixing her glasses.

"Morning. I would like to open an account."

"Oh okay. Have you had an account with us before?" she asked, wondering if he was wearing makeup or if his skin was just fucked up.

Before he could even reply, there was a loud scream.

"Ahhh Ahhh! Oh my God! My baby!" a pregnant woman yelled, leaning on the countertop where the bank deposit slips were located.

Civilians, the security guard, and a couple of bank tellers ran to the woman's aid who looked like she was about to give labor.

"Here you go," Black said, passing the bank teller a note that read:

"Give me everything in your drawer and under the counter in the small safe. No dye or GPS systems or your son dies. My goons are outside of his daycare on Field Street."

The bank teller almost had tears in her eyes with a contemplative look on her face. When she saw his gun under his blazer pointed at her, she did what he asked real quick.

In less than ten seconds, Black had a bag full of money sliding out the side door while everybody paid attention to the pregnant woman who thought her water broke, but it was a false alarm.

***

Fifteen minutes later, Black parked the old Honda in Sam's Club parking lot, waiting for someone ready to get the fuck outta Delaware before the police are all over the place.

Black waited in line behind a certain amount of people so he could go to the fat black bitch's window. He'd been tailing her for two days and every day after work she went to pick up her son from his daycare center on Field Street.

He knew it was a dexterous plan and she wouldn't try anything to risk the life of her son even though he was lying about his goons being outside the daycare center.

When he saw a gray Kia pull up, he wiped down the Honda with cleaning wipes to get rid of his fingerprints. He grabbed the money and hopped out, leaving the car there.

"Hey babe," Black said, kissing his wifey's lips.

"How I do?" she asked, pulling out the fake pregnant stomach she brought from online.

"Amazing. Did they call the police?"

"No. When I saw you leave, I got up off the floor and left, baby," she said turning on to the highway and heading back to the Bronx.

Black's wifey, Katrina, was a sexy, thick, brown chick from the Bronx. She was an ex-scammer, but now with children, she was focused on taking care of her babies. She would sometimes help Black, like in situations like today, when he needed a distraction.

"I'ma make love to you all night, baby, on top of the money," he said.

"Umm… I can't wait," Katrina said as his finger slid in her wet and tight pussy.

***

Yonkers, NY

Today was Thanksgiving and Andy just had dinner with his grandma, dad, and girl, Erica, at his house on Elm Street. Erica was in the kitchen helping his grandma wash dishes and clean up.

Andy just got off the phone with his man from Jackson Street telling his about some Mexican kingpin nigga who was an MS-13.

Andy needed a lick and it seemed as if it just fell in his lap. He didn't give a fuck about who you knew or ran with. If you were moving big weight in Yonkers, he was coming for it.

He knew the MS-13 gang had a trail of bodies around the city two summers ago. It was a lot of them on the Southside, but Andy didn't give a fuck. He was making plans to do his research and homework on them.

Romell Tukes

Chapter 14

Yonkers, NY
Weeks Later

It was 11:37 pm and Wolf was parked across the street of Champ's baby mother's building on Riverdale. Champ was upstairs in his baby mother's crib spending time with his family.

Wolf had one of the best hacking skills in the city, he could basically hack into anything with internet access. His sister, Victoria, was ten times better than him. She was a computer whiz.

When he saw Champ and his baby mother hop out of a new Jaguar, he ran the license plate by hacking into the DMV system. The plates to the Jag were under the name Shayla Davis and the address was 75 Riverdale Avenue, Apartment #3C Yonkers, NY 10701. He even saw a picture of Shayla and she was the woman with Champ earlier.

Wolf watched the building closely. It was freezing outside today and New Year's Eve, so it was a snowy New York night.

Since killing Fred, he had been laying low at home, helping his mom around the house and building with Bella. They were now into a real serious relationship. Fred's killing was all over the Westchester news. The news reporter claimed they never saw such a gruesome murder.

Champ came walking out the building with a bottle of Henny in his hand and a bookbag in his other hand. Wolf felt the blood rush to his head as he watched Champ climb in the Jaguar and drive off. Once the Jaguar was out of his rearview, Wolf made his way to the apartment building in a precipitous manner because it was below five degrees outside.

Inside, he took the stairs to the third floor to preclude and prevent him from being seen by any resident living in the building. He pulled his hoodie over his head and pulled out his .9mm pistol. Wolf knocked twice and heard someone behind the door.

"I thought you was going out..." Shayla said, smiling and showing her big brown eyes. She was excited, thinking her boo was coming back to bring in the New Year with her and the kids.

Shayla looked at Wolf thinking he had the wrong apartment, but when he raised his gun to her head, she almost choked on her own spit.

"Shhhhh... Go into the living room," Wolf said, walking into the apartment to hear loud music playing in the stereo system.

"Please my kids are in the back, Champ just left" she cried sitting down on her living room couch in tears.

"Your baby father chose your family's fate," Wolf said, walking over to the stereo surround sound system and turning it up to the full max.

"Please, I'll do whatever. I'll give you his mom, sister, and side bitch's info. They all live on Elliot Street!" she shouted over the music.

Pop! Pop! Pop!

Wolf placed three shots into her head, leaving her head hanging off the back of the couch and forming a puddle of blood on the carpet.

Wolf then walked to the back of the clean apartment. He saw a door with kid drawings on the door confirming it was a kid's room as he opened the door.

He saw a bunk bed with a boy and girl in deep sleep. With no remorse, he fired two rounds into both of the kids, but before he turned to leave, he pulled out a picture of Victoria and placed it on the cartoon carpet.

Wolf left like a mouse at night creeping through the projects.

***

Five Points Prison
One Month Later

"Mr. Lambert, you have a lot of money on your release account. Let me guess, you were in here selling drugs with your Blood homies." This big, white C.O. with Nazi tattoos all over his arms was in his feelings looking at the enormous amount of money.

"Nah, we had your wife selling pussy to all the inmates," Smurf said with a laugh.

The C.O. looked at him like he was ready to knock out his teeth.

"You got a smart mouth on you, boy. I know you'll be back, and I'll be waiting for you just like we waited for Monster," the C.O. said, looking at Smurf's face turn sour.

Monster was a big homie Blood from the Bronx. He was causing hell in Five Points and all over the state prisons. Monster went home and caught a sixty-day violation coming back to Five Points. The correctional officers killed him in the box also known as the special housing unit. They made his murder look like suicide.

"Suck a dick," Smurf said, grabbing his personal property which was an iPhone, a wallet, I.D. cards, and a Cuban link necklace.

"See you later," the guard said laughing while two other C.O.'s led Smurf out of the prison. Today was his release day; it was the best feeling in the world.

Smurf wore a thick, red, and white Dolce Gabbana sweatsuit with a crispy new pair of wheat colored Timbs that Shantell sent him two weeks ago.

Stepping outside the gates it was snowy outside, the snow stood up to five to seven inches.

"Baby!" Shantell shouted, running into his arms.

"Damn ma, I just saw you last week"

"Shut up," she said wiping her tears.

"Come on ma. Let's get out of here before I kill one of these guards in this bitch."

"I hope you like this Papi."

"Like what?" he said, looking at Shantell point at a red Range Rover Sport. It was brand new with tints and black rims.

"Wow, babe! Thank you," he said kissing her soft lips moving her long hair out the way.

"I knew you would like it. Andy said you wouldn't," she said, climbing in the driver's seat.

"Where he at?"

"Getting shit ready at Club Cityscapes in Queens for your welcome home party," she said, pulling off.

"Okay party tonight because I gotta report to my parole officer in New Rochelle on Monday and I heard she's a real bitch," he said seriously.

"Well, you're staying out of trouble this time. You've got wild money, a bad bitch, and a plan. I can't lose you again to this jail shit, daddy. You mean too much to me," she said, emotionally because, for his whole time gone, she never had a good night's sleep.

She did her from time to time, but it was nothing serious and only a nut because Smurf was the only nigga that she could fully give herself to. Niggas was too much of a headache nowadays anyway and they always came with extra baggage.

"Don't worry about nothing, ma. We litty, so just chill," he said, seeing a rest stop area. "Pull over in there."

"For what Papi? We got a full tank," she said.

"I'm trying to see what that pussy hitting on, ma. I'm horny as hell."

"In the rest stop?" she asked nervously.

"Hell yeah! Let's get it in the restroom for a quickie," he said.

Shantell parked and followed him into the restroom and locked the door. The restroom smelled like piss and was dirty, but Smurf ain't care. He dropped his sweatpants and Shantell got on her knees, sucking his dick, and getting it wet.

"Mmmm... ssss..." he moaned while she deep throated him, slobbering all over his dick. He had to stop her because he wasn't trying to embarrass himself from her elite head game.

He bent her over on the sink, sliding down her stretchy jeans and panties. He entered her from behind, feeling her wetness dripping out her tiny hole.

"Ugh shittt, Papi! Yesss!" Shantell cried out because he was pounding her pussy out like a madman.

"Damn," Smurf grunted, pumping in and out of her, slapping his pelvis on her big soft ass that jiggled with ripples every time he slammed his dick into her...

"Shitttt..." he shouted out of breath and cumming inside of her. When he pulled out, she turned around with the quickness to see his dick went limp.

"That's it?" she said with a disgusted look on her face as she watched him get dressed.

"Baby, I'm fresh out of jail. Give me a couple of days to shoot off my blanks, then shit will be back to regular.

"It better be, nigga, or your ass is going to be replaced. Shit, I ain't wait three hard years for no trash ass dick. You better talk to your third leg and bring the old Smurf out," she said, getting dressed.

The ride to Shantell's crib in the Bronx went smoothly. Smurf got ready for his party in a couple of hours at the strip club. It felt so good to finally be free.

Romell Tukes

Chapter 15

Yonkers, NY
Weeks Later

Andy and Smurf were parked at the end of the block, watching the Mexican restaurant attached to the dry cleaners.

"Where you get this car from? It smells like dog piss," Smurf said, looking around the old Cadillac.

"A crackhead, nigga. Where else?"

"Are you sure about this lick, bro? You know how these niggas get down," Smurf said, hoping his best friend would change his mind about running up in the spot to get at a Mexican plug.

"Bro, anybody can get it. Money ain't got no face or race, homie. You know how we get down. If this shit backfires, we go to war, bro," Andy said.

"A'ight. I'm with you. It's go time?"

"Nah, in seven minutes. When they lock up, then we'll go through the back exit.

"How we getting in?"

"A nigga takes out the garbage at the same time every night, so that's our way inside," Andy said, sounding like a GPS system.

Andy had been plotting this lick out for two months, ever since he got the call from his Voda Loco homie, Chopper. That nigga put him on to a kingpin nigga named Ortiz.

"What's up with your parole officer?"

"Bro, she's a bad white bitch and I can tell she wants the dick," Smurf said.

"A'ight, nigga. That's what you think until she locks your ass up," Andy added.

"Man, them bitches got emotions under that tough skin, but she let me do whatever. The only thing she stressed was to not have the police contact her for anything and come in every Wednesday."

"Let's roll," Andy said, checking his rose gold Audemars Piguet Royal Oak Chronograph watch.

Smurf and Andy pulled their masks over their faces and grabbed the two pistols with thirty-round clips.

***

Ortiz was ready to head home to his wife and get some sleep. It was a long Friday. He owned the Mexican restaurant and the dry cleaners next door. Ortiz was the nephew of a very powerful man named Jimenez; he was a Blackhand, which was a powerful Mexican gang leader. Ortiz's brother, Sousa, was a kingpin under his Uncle Jimenez who was from Cali but living in New York.

At thirty years old, Ortiz had everything any man could ask for, the riches, the mansion, the beautiful wife, and the luxury lifestyle. Ortiz sold keys of heroin and his brother sold coke. He had two stash spots one was inside of a broken dryer in his laundromat and the other was in his Long Island home. He didn't live in Yonkers anymore where he grew up on the southside. He was a high-ranking MS-13 gang member just like his brother. Their turf was all over the southside of Yonkers where they controlled the drug trade.

It was past midnight and Ortiz grabbed the trash to take it out as he did every night before he went home. When he took the trash out to the back dumpster, two men popped out on him with guns drawn.

"Don't make no funny moves or I'ma blow your fucking head clean off. Now, walk back inside," Smurf said, feeling like his old self. This was his first robbery since being home and the rush it gave him made him remember why he loved robbing niggas.

Ortiz walked back inside into the kitchen scared for his life, he had never been robbed or held at gunpoint because of who his family was. He wasn't the killer type; he was more of the businessman type.

"Sit on the floor," Andy said, sitting in front of him taking off his mask.

"This must be a mistake," Ortiz said.

"Oh no, it's not. Ortiz, where is the dope? We're not here to play games" Andy said.

"Okay, I want no trouble. Everything is in the laundry mat. Go to dryer six and take off the front door frame," Ortiz said. Smurf made his way towards the laundry mat while Andy kept a close eye on Ortiz who was staring at him with puppy dog eyes.

"Papi, you don't know what you're doing. Those drugs belong to powerful people. I'm the middleman," Ortiz stated, trying to save Andy's life.

"Shut the fuck up!"

Minutes later Smurf came back into the restaurant dragging a black Hefty garbage bag filled with bricks and money.

"Yo this nigga had the motherload, son," Smurf said, sweating under his mask because it was hot and humid in the kitchen.

"We would let you live, but I think you know that's not happening," Andy said before he and Smurf filled his body up with twenty-two bullets.

***

Across town, College Avenue

Bella made the police force a couple of weeks ago and she was proud of herself. Tonight, she was working the night shift which most cops called the graveyard shift because most of the murders took place at night.

Her partner, Officer Kingston, was a white cop, in his mid-thirties. He'd been on the force for eight years with a long resume of harassing civilians. He was a real asshole.

The patrol car stopped at a red. Listening to their walkie-talkie, a call came in about a trespassing taking place a block away.

"That's us," Kingston said, flashing on his lights and making a left up the hill. Yonkers was filled with hills and in the wintertime, it was the worst. Most calls they wouldn't even show up unless it was a 187 or 207 a robbery in process.

Bella saw a teenager in a hoodie and peacoat walk away from the building in a rush.

"Aye, you! Stop!" Kingston yelled, but the teenager turned around seeing it was Kingston, and took off running in fear.

Kingston and Bella took off after him, but when Kingston was close enough, he tased him, dropping the teen. Kingston didn't stop there, he started to pistol whip the teen as he started screaming and blood flew everywhere.

"Kingston, stop! You're going to kill him!" Bella yelled. She couldn't believe what she was witnessing.

"Fucking punk!" Kingston spit, kicking him in his stomach before walking off. "Come on. Our job is done," Kinston said, walking off.

Bella wanted to help the young man, but Kingston kept calling her name, so she turned to leave.

"What was that all about?" she asked.

"He shouldn't have run and he looked like he was going to pull something out," he said, pulling off.

"What?"

"Look, Bella, you gotta get with the program and realize where the fuck you at," he said ending the conversation.

Bella said nothing else. she just shook her head in deep thought.

Chapter 16

White Plains, NY

Champ was driving on his way back to Yonkers from visiting Shayla's mom and family. Everyone was devastated over her and the kids' deaths.

On New Year's day, Champ came home early in the morning to see his high school sweetheart with bullet wounds to her head. When he went to check on his kids, he fell on his knees crying over the loud music that was playing since he left for a New Year's Eve party across town.

Champ couldn't figure out who would be so cold-blooded to kill a nigga's kids. He had so much beef over the years with the killers and it could have been anybody, but he did have a couple of people in mind and the first was Andy.

***

Yonkers, NY

Wolf recently got an apartment on North Boulevard. It was a nice little one-bedroom for $900 a month just to get out of his mom's house. Everything was good at home, but since the death of his sister, his mother had been acting very strange and different. Rita walked around the house depressed all day, not taking showers, calling out from work, and letting herself go. Wolf had to find a source of income soon because he had to pay rent and his car insurance every month.

"Baby, you gotta get ready. We have to meet my father for dinner in the city," Bella said, walking out of his bathroom in a black dress and heels with her hair in a bun.

"I know, love. I'm about to take a shower and get ready. Calm down, you making me nervous," he said, grabbing her waist and bringing her between his legs.

"I just want this to go good. You're my second boyfriend that I ever had and the first to introduce to my father, so this is big," she said seriously.

"Chill ma. We're good."

"You and this chill shit," she said, walking off into the living room.

Bella and Wolf spent a lot of time together. She would spend the night sometimes, so she can go to work. They were both in love with each other and very happy.

Wolf took a shower and got dressed in a Tom Ford suit, looking very mature and wealthy. He was far from rich; he couldn't even afford a full gas tank in his car.

When they got on the road, she could tell something was wrong with him. She saw his gas tank was a quarter full.

"You want to go and get some gas? I got it," she said.

"Nah, babe. It's cool. I'll take care of it. I didn't even realize it," he said, lying and not trying to let her know he was really hurting.

"Romeo, you can ask me for anything. I'm not that type of chick. What's mine is yours, baby," she said.

"I know. Thank you. How's work? You were telling me something earlier, but I was half asleep. You know you got that knockout." He chuckled.

"You so stupid... The other day at work, we got a call somewhere and a black teen was minding his business. When he saw Kingston, my partner, he took off like a track star, so we ran after him."

"These hoodlums got my baby running," Wolf added.

"Would you listen? So, Kingston gets him down on the floor and starts to pistol-whip him."

"So, what you do?" Wolf said, knowing she was better than that.

"I stopped him, babe, but the fire I'd seen in his eyes was as if he wanted to kill the kid. It freaked me out. I even had a dream about the shit," she said pensively.

"You're going to be faced with a lot of challenges as a cop out here. Make sure you stick to your morals and guns. Don't let them change you for who you are, babe," he said.

"I know. It's just crazy how they treat blacks out here," she stated.

"It's not just out here, it's everywhere," he said, driving to Manhattan. He was speeding, hoping to beat the snowstorm that was to come later.

***

Manhattan, NY

Wolf and Bella walked into the dim restaurant to see Bella's father waiting for them in the crowded place.

"Daddy…" Bella said, hugging her father.

"Hey beautiful, so this is Romeo?" Aguilera said. He began looking Wolf up and down, sizing him up to see if he was Spanish.

"It's a pleasure to meet you, Mr. Aguilera. I heard so much about you, sir," Wolf said, shaking his hand.

"Oh, you have? Well, my baby girl has always had a big mouth," he said, laughing as everybody was seated. "You Spanish?" he asked Wolf.

"Yes, sir. I'm Dominican and Black," Wolf stated.

"Good, good. Your name is very unique. Just don't break my daughter's heart. She really likes you."

"Dad, it's too early for that," Bella said looking at the food menu.

"What's your plan now that you finished school, young man?" Aguilera asked.

"I'm getting my thoughts together now, but I want to open my own law firm," Wolf said.

"Excuse me, I have to go to the little girls' room … play nice, daddy," Bella said, getting up from the table.

"Your sister was recently killed, I'm sorry to hear that."

"Yeah, she had a bright future," Wolf replied.

"You have any dealing with them, hoodlums, on Elm Street."

"No sir, but that's where I'm from."

"I know they call you, Wolf, right?" Aguilera asked.

"Yeah. How did you know?"

"You're fucking my daughter; I have to know everything about you. I'm an FBI Agent, so I have access to everything. Take this piece of paper and meet me there next Monday. Be sure to keep this between us," Aguilera said, seeing Bella come back to the table.

"What's going on? Don't stop talking now," she said.

"I'm just getting to know Romeo a little better," her father said before they ordered their food and enjoyed the day.

Chapter 17

Auburn Maximum-Security Prison

Rita was in the visiting room waiting on her son to come out. She came up here to visit CB four times a year, but she would send money orders monthly and a thirty-five-pound food package every other month.

After losing Victoria, she had to take time to regain control over herself because losing her only daughter took a lot out of her. Rita was slowly coming back together; she was back at work driving school buses and back at the nursing home driving the elders around.

Winter was starting to break, so spring was right around the corner. She had plans to get back in the gym. Rita was still beautiful with her youthful, flawless skin and amazing body, she turned heads at forty-five years old.

CB walked out from the back with other inmates coming out to visit their families. His big muscles were bulging out his collared shirt and his box braids were hanging down his face.

"Mom," CB said, hugging his mom tightly and not wanting to let her go. He hadn't seen her in months. The last time was a month before his little sister's murder.

"Sorry, I ain't come up here sooner. Vicky's death took a toll on me."

"I know mom. It fucked me up," CB said, looking into his mom's bright hazel eyes. He was glad that she was okay because he was worried about her. CB was the oldest and he knew his mom could shut down at times.

"How are you doing in this hell hole? I hate that you're in here, baby. You didn't deserve this," she said sadly.

"I'm okay. Due to the circumstances, I'm just doing my time like a soldier with my head high."

"Good. That's what mommy likes to hear. When is your next parole hearing? Or parole board, whatever they call that shit," she said.

"In a couple of years, but with the life on the end they can hit me every two years until I grow old in this bitch."

"Think positive and stay in your prayers. Where there is a will there's a way," she stated.

"Facts. What's going on with my brothers?"

"Well, I don't speak to Black. His ass is a disgrace to this family."

"Mom, don't say that," CB added. He knew how Black was, but he was still family.

"He didn't even show up to his own sister's funeral and that says a lot," she said, seriously.

"Damn, I ain't know that."

"Yeah, he still be up to no good, robbing them banks. I don't want him to brainwash your little brother, so I keep him far away from that devil."

"How is Wolf?"

"He just recently graduated from college with his Criminal Justice degree."

"I'm happy for him. He has always been clever."

"Shit too clever, but he got a nice beautiful Puerto Rican girlfriend who's a cop."

"Oh yeah? Damn, he doing it like that?"

"Yeah and he got his own crib, but I barely see him nowadays. His birthday was yesterday and Black's," she said.

"I know. You still exercising, or you took time off?" CB asked, knowing his mom was a health nut just like him.

"I've taken off, but I'm about to turn this thing up. I plan to hit a lot of beaches this summer."

"Mmmmm, I don't need no more little brothers or sisters."

"Shit don't be surprised. Mama got that waterfall. These young boys be out here chasing," she said, laughing.

"I ain't trying to hear that," CB said.

When the visit ended, she promised to come back and visit soon.

***

CB got back to D-Block just in time for count time. He saw OG chuck was sleeping in his cell next door.

CB took an hour nap then woke up, brushed his teeth, used the bathroom, and prepared for chow time in the mess hall.

When his unit was called for chow, OG pulled up on his as they walked in a single file line to the prison dining room mess hall area to eat dinner.

"How was your visit?" OG asked

"Some old mama love. She pulled up on a nigga."

"Oh, okay. Good to take you out of jail for a while."

"Facts. But why everybody moving funny?" CB said seeing the looks on everybody's faces walking past.

"A Muslim kid from Rochester stabbed up a Puerto Rican nigga from the Bronx over some dope earlier on the handball court. The shit almost caused a race riot, but the Bloods were looking for you earlier. I believe they got something going on," OG said walking into the packed kitchen.

The mess hall was silent today every time this happened there was a lot of tension in the air.

CB and OG sat at the table in the back full of Bloods and Brooklyn niggas.

"CB, we got a problem, hot boy," J Brim said, sitting across from CB.

"Talk Skrap."

"The new homie that just got here was caught fucking the tranny in the kitchen warehouse."

"What... Nigga, what homie?" P Hat was shocked.

"The light skin nigga?"

"Yeah, he got caught fucking the Spanish punk with the ass and titties."

"The one who looks like J Lo?" CB asked.

"Yeah, son. The same nigga who got caught fucking with the Ape from Yonkers," J Brim said trying to be funny but serious.

"That nigga not from Yonkers. But who caught son and did y'all speak to the mook?"

"A Latin King nigga who work back there walked in on him busting son's back open. We pulled up on the punk and he told it all. Them niggas been fucking since they were in Wendy's prison and even Bare Hill," P Hat said, eating his meatloaf on his tray.

"Where he at now?" CB asked.

"He's sitting with the homies in the front. They're rocking Boy to sleep, but he wanted to speak to you first. He heard what's poppin."

"I ain't got shit to talk about with that nigga. That's a double O, Skrap. Tell Lil Murda from Harlem to take that deal and send the shooter, Brim, as his safety. Tell them niggas they better not fumble or they both out of here."

"A'ight."

"I want son out the spot on the first. Go back and tell them to rip both sides of his face," CB said, getting ready to leave with OG.

"Got you, Brim strong."

"Brim firm," CB said, walking off pissed. These niggas were making his gang look bad by fucking gay niggas.

"You cooking tonight?" OG asked.

"Yeah. What you in the mood for, old head?"

"You're only good at seafood coconut rice."

"Got jokes, but a'ight. I got you," CB said, walking through the hall back to the block.

Anytime there was a problem with the Bloods everybody went to CB. Because he had the jail and with over a hundred Bloods in his set, he was always busy with other people's issues.

Chapter 18

Ossining, NY

Ra Ra stood outside of his auto body shop talking to one of his workers, about overcharging clients on paint jobs.

"If it happens again, Rob, your ass is fired," Ra Ra said, walking off.

Ra Ra was moving keys of heroin in Upper Westchester County where he opened an auto body shop with the money he saved up. He got his starter kit three years ago when Smurf got locked up. Smurf was his little cousin who was doing big things in Yonkers by robbing big-time drug dealers.

When Smurf got locked up his girlfriend reached out to Ra Ra with a plan and he agreed to rob his own cousin

Ra Ra linked up with Danielle and robbed Smurf's crib, which was a small studio room full of drugs and money from Smurf's previous robberies.

That same night, Ra Ra and Danielle had sex and they've been fucking ever since. Ra Ra had no remorse for what he did. He respected the game and he heard Smurf had caught a thirty-year bid, so he thought he was doing his little cousin a favor.

He got inside of white Land Range Rover Evoque. He began driving down the street on his way to the Bronx to meet his Jamaican plug who had the best heroin right now around the city. Ra Ra stopped at a red light, pulling up next to a red Honda CLX sports bike. His phone was ringing, but he couldn't find it until he reached under his seat. When he answered the phone, he thought he was hearing shit, or it was a prank call.

"I'm going to kill you..." the caller said, mocking the *Scream* movie.

"Man, who the fuck is this?" Ra Ra was looking at his window to see the nigga on the bike on the phone with his helmet lifted. When Ra Ra saw his face, he hit the gas. However, he was not fast enough.

Smurf lifted the Tech 9, rattling Ra Ra's body with bullets. Thirty rounds blew before popping his clutch on his bike and racing off down the street on a wheelie, making the bike roar.

***

Nyack, NY

Smurf pulled up to the building Shantell gave him where his ex-girlfriend, Danielle, lived. Word was Danielle recently had a baby by a dope boy from Rockland County.

Smurf knew Danielle since the first grade, and they were close. So, when he heard what she did, he couldn't believe it. Every night for three years, what she did was a constant replay in his mind. He waited for this day for years.

From what he heard, Danielle worked at Foot Locker in the Palisades Center Mall, minutes away from Nyack. Word was she spent all the money she stole from on her body and shopping sprees. The dumb bitch had nothing to show for it unlike Ra Ra, who invested his money into an auto body shop.

Smurf saw an old Honda Accord with two donuts on the tires and a plastic bag taped to the back window.

***

Danielle parked her hooptie in her parking spot ready to go pick up her son from her neighbor who looked after him when she went to work. Her baby father put a seed in her and left for Ohio to get money, leaving her broke and helpless after selling her dreams.

She was Haitian and Dominican, thick, tatted, light skin, short, and a dime piece. Danielle had only been regretting everything she did to him. Once she heard he caught thirty years, everything went out the window.

"You're in a rush, Danielle," Smurf said, walking behind her. When she heard his voice, she stopped at a nick of a dime.

"Oh my God, Smurf!" she said with tears quickly rolling down her high cheekbones.

"Thought I was going to forget, bitch?"

"Smurf, I'm sorry," she said, seeing the big machine gun with air holes in the barrel.

"Too late, hoe..."

Tat-tat-tat-tat-tat!

Smurf spit on her dead body when it hit the floor, then hopped back on his bike doing donuts out the lot. Smurf loved motorcycles. He was one of the best stuntmen in Yonkers and the Bronx. He was even placed in two magazines for his bike skills.

***

Midtown, NY

Wolf parked at the small riverfront on the Hudson River in the middle of the city to meet Bella's dad here for whatever reason.

There were businessmen and women out walking around on their lunch break. Wolf saw Mr. Aguilera sit down on a bench on the walkway and he started feeding the birds.

Wolf took a deep breath and made his way to Bella's dad trying to wrap his mind around what was to come.

"Romeo or would you like me to call you Wolf?" Aguilera said with a smirk.

"Whatever is good for you."

"Okay. Wolf, it is. Have a seat, please, young man."

"What's going on Mr. Aguilera?" Wolf asked sensing something was off with him.

"Call me Aguilera for now on unless my daughter is present. You and I have a lot in common, Wolf."

"How's that, sir? I don't know shit about you," Wolf said, getting irritated with the games.

"You see that's where you're wrong. You will only know what I tell you about me, but I know everything about you," Aguilera said, passing him a brown envelope.

Wolf looked in the envelope to see pictures of himself dragging Fred's body into a factory and more pictures of him dragging out Fred's dead body, tossing it into a Cadillac, and driving off. He also had photos of him entering Shayla's apartment building. Photos of him entering her home with a gun. He also saw news clips of the gruesome murders.

"You should have been a photographer or paparazzi, but that's not me. You have the wrong guy, sorry," Wolf said.

"So clever, but so dumb. You killed all those people in retaliation for your sister's murder. Wolf, you were a good kid until that happened, but this could get you life in prison. Shit, maybe even the chair," Aguilera said seriously.

"What do you want?"

"I want to give you a way out for my little girl's sake. When she used to come home talking about you, I wanted to do my own research on you. When Bella told me about your sister, I was saddened for you. That's when I started to watch you to make sure you were good for my baby. After I saw what you did to Fred, I saw why they call you Wolf. You have no friends, no real family, only my daughter."

"Can you get to the point?"

"You will be going on missions for me until I say so and if you don't, I will nail you to the fucking ground so hard you'll be scared of daylight," Aguilera said, staring into his eyes.

"What if I get knocked?"

"Don't worry about that. I'm a Federal Agent, so I got you. I just need you to be smart because the people you're going to kill are powerful people. I'm getting paid big money for these hits, so don't fuck up! The first mission is two Mexicans."

"So, I'm your personal hitman under a blackmail agreement?"

"Yes, you have no choice, but whatever you find is yours. Here is your first victim. Don't look at it here, but I'll be in touch. I'm sure you got guns," Aguilera said, leaving.

Chapter 19

Yonkers, NY

"This dope is moving, son. Every morning, niggas is knocking off a key," Lil Tom said. He was posted up on Elm Street and London in front of the corner store with Andy.

"I already know my guy just make sure y'all cut that shit right or niggas going be dropping," Andy said, eating a bacon, egg, and cheese sandwich.

"Shit, niggas get high at your own risk. That's why we used the cautious sign as our stamps," Lil tom said, watching six of his little homies run up and down the block passing off bundles of heroin to fiends.

"What's good with your brother, Trigger? I heard he down south getting to a big bag."

"That nigga doing it big. He got a plug down there under his wing, but we don't really talk that much," Lil Tom said.

"Nigga, you sold all his guns!"

"Better for me to sell them than for the police to find them shits and at my mom's house."

"So that's your excuse?"

"I'm sticking to it."

"Grimy little nigga," Andy said, laughing.

"What poppin with that plug from the Heights that you met at the dice game?"

"I'm supposed to go downtown to chop it up with him today. Both me and Smurf because niggas need a plug. Fuck all this free-lancing shit," Andy said, seeing two of Lil Tom's young boys jump a fiend in front of a building.

"Let me go get these niggas. They making shit hot," Lil Tom said, spinning off. Andy had to go pick up Smurf from the Bronx, so he hopped in his Benz pulling off.

***

Southside, Yonkers

Chopper walked into the close Mexican bar to meet Crazy. Over twenty MS-13 Mexicans were surrounding the bar with mean faces. Chopper was an MS-18 gangbanger. He didn't really fuck with the MS-13 gang, who were his rivals. Chopper put Andy on to Ortiz for a piece of the pie, but Andy went against his word and didn't give Chopper a penny. When he tried to call Andy, he changed his number on him.

Word on the street was Crazy had twenty-thousand large for any information on his brother's murder, so this was his chance to get even. Crazy's guards patted him down to see that he was clean.

"Crazy, nice to meet you. They call me Chopper."

"I know who you are, so fuck the small talk. What do you have for me?" Crazy said in his cold eyes with MS tattoos covering his face and bald head.

Crazy looked like he was from Cali, but he was from Long Island where the MS-13 ran the city and Yonkers was their second turf.

"I know who killed your brother," Chopper said as Crazy sat up straight.

"I hope you know anything you say, your life will depend on it," Crazy said, staring into Chopper's eyes.

"I know, but I'm 100% sure who did it because he came to me trying to sell me keys of heroin for a low price. When I asked him where he gets it from, he said that he killed Ortiz."

"Who?"

"Andy, a nigger from Elm Street."

"So, you're telling me the Blacks did this to my brother?"

"Yes, I can put my life on it. We're Mexican, bro. We gotta look out for each other," Chopper said as Crazy leaned back. Both Crazy and Chopper knew that this could lead to a big war in Yonkers.

"I have $10,000 for you now and when I get to the bottom of this, I will pay you the other ten for your services."

"Okay, thank you," Chopper said. He got up to leave after one of Crazy's guards handed him the ten bands.

"Chopper?"

"Yeah?" Chopper said, stopping at the door on his way out.

"If I find out you had something to do with this or your story don't add up, I'ma kill you and your whole family," Crazy said seriously.

Chopper said nothing and walked out with noodle legs and a rapid heartbeat.

***

Wilton, Long Island

Crazy walked into his uncle's mansion which was a Polynesian-style home with an antique setting from the doors, wallpaper and furniture, and antique wide pine floors.

Goons were all over the place to protect his uncle who was a very powerful man from California. He was a part of the Blackhand organization, a large group of powerful Mexicans.

Crazy took the stairs to the second-floor library where his uncle spent most of his time when he was in New York.

Crazy walked into the library to see his uncle doing a puzzle.

"Loco perfect timing," Jimenez said, taking off his big reading glasses trying to figure out the big puzzle in front of him. "You was always good at puzzles and chess, the two best games for the mind," Jimenez said.

Crazy uncle called him Loco which was Crazy in Spanish. Crazy sat down to help his uncle with a puzzle.

Jimenez was in his sixties and a very powerful man from South Central. He had two other brothers who were also Blackhands. Jimenez served twenty-seven years at San Quentin prison in California where he became a Blackhand. He wore a thick mustache, short, husky, and was very calm and humble.

"I believe I have a lead on Ortiz's murder."

"Good. Who was it? I bet you it was them MS-18 fools," Jimenez stated.

"No, it was the Blacks," Crazy said as Jimenez stopped and looked up at him

"You're positive because if so, this could be big?"
"I'm positive, but I'm doing my research now."
"Okay just keep it clean and quick."
"I will," Crazy said, ending the conversation and helping his uncle with the puzzle.

Chapter 20

Newburgh, NY

"Thanks for coming up here with me, babe. I gotta come up here once a month to practice on my shooting. Every cop does now since they made it a law for law enforcement," Bella said looking on to the highway up the 9A route.

"Y'all cops don't need to be working on shooting shit. Y'all need communication skills," Wolf said, halfway joking, but Bella found nothing funny.

"What do you mean y'all? I'm a normal person, Romeo. Don't label me," she said, feeling insulted by his cruel remark.

'I didn't mean it like that Bella, at all. I'm sorry."

"It's okay, but you know I'm trying to make a big difference. Yesterday, I went to a couple of schools around Yonkers to speak to the youth. Guess what a little boy asked me?"

"What?"

"Are you going to shoot us?" she said, shaking her head in disbelief.

"Damn, I know that shit fucked you up."

"Hell, yeah. When I asked him why he asked that, he said because he saw police kill his father for nothing in their home," Bella said.

"I feel his pain. I just hope he can see past that growing up because I saw a lot of kids fall victim from the things they saw growing up," Wolf said, getting off the Newburgh exit near the shopping centers and restaurants.

"How come you never talk about your father or your childhood?" she asked a question that she'd been wanting to bring up.

"I don't know my father, but I know he is Dominican and Mexican. When I used to go to DR as a kid and teen to my aunt's house, she used to tell me little stories. However, my mom never talked about him," Wolf said, pulling into the gun range parking lot.

"I'm sorry."

"For what?"

"That you had to experience that feeling because when my mom died, I felt alone, depressed, hopeless and like a knife ripped through my heart," she said seriously.

"You don't have to feel like that no more because you got me."

"I know," she said, grabbing her work bag with her work gun and her personal gun she just brought days ago.

"Are you sure I can get in here? It's a police shooting range," Wolf said seeing cops walk in and out.

"It's open to the public on weekends and as long as you have no felonies, you're okay. Come on, stop acting so scared. I want to teach you how to shoot anyway," she said climbing out of the car in her police sweatsuit.

"Whatever you say," Wolf said, following her inside the huge gun range.

The people at the front desk ran his name to make sure he wasn't a convict. When he was clear, they let him pick some guns to use for target practice.

Bella grabbed a Glock 9mm with seventeen shots and a Glock 40. Wolf grabbed an AK-47 with fifty shots and a Colt 45 handgun with extra clips.

"Are you sure you can handle that?" Bella asked.

"I can teach you a thing or two."

"Romeo, please. This isn't your PlayStation 4, boo."

"Okay, we will see," Wolf said, putting on his headphones and thick glasses for protection.

Bella went into the booth first, firing at the target sheet until the Glock 9mm was empty and jammed.

"Beat that," Bella said, taking off her glasses and headphones. She pressed a button so another target sheet can appear for him.

Wolf went into the small booth, aimed his Colt 45, shooting round after round into the sheet until he was done.

"Too easy," he said, switching out with her again.

"You just made it look easy, but I don't think you even hit the paper," she said laughing pressing a button to receive a new sheet for her.

Bella grabbed her .40 and began shooting at her target which was now a picture of a human body. When she was finished, Wolf went using his AK-47 on his sheet spraying fifty rounds. Bella knew there was no way in hell Wolf hit his target with all of those rounds.

"Let's check the score sheet. It's on the computer," Bella said, typing in her booth number to see their results.

"Okay, here it is. I shot a 62% on the first target and the second target my shooting was 72% which is good shooting," she said, sticking out her tongue. She was listening to the loud shooting coming from other booths at the range.

"Check my shit," Wolf said.

"Your first target was 98%... What?" Bella said, confused. "That can't be," she said, shocked.

"Check the other one."

"It says 100%, Romeo. Wow, this is crazy. How is that even possible?"

"When I was a kid, my aunt trained me in shooting and fighting using martial arts skills," he said, thinking back to when he used to go to the Dominican Republic with his aunt on his father's side every summer for eighteen years.

"What kind of aunt do you have?"

"You don't want to know," Wolf replied. He began loading back up the weapons and teaching Bella how to shoot correctly, standing behind her.

***

Yonkers, NY
Days Later

Andy's heroin was moving so fast, he had to expand across town to a dead-end block on Avon Place, which was a gold mine for heroin.

It was late and he was on his way home to the new crib he got with Erica last week on Maple Street.

Things had been great he had been dealing with Flaco, the new plug that he recently met. The keys he stole from Ortiz were almost gone. Luckily, Flaco's dope was good, but not as good as Ortiz. It got the job done, nevertheless.

Andy lit a cigarette before walking to his Benz parked at the end of the thin narrow street.

He walked past a big van with tints, but Andy didn't remember seeing the van earlier. He just dropped off six bricks of dope to his homie Sick-O, so he was clean just in case it was the police lurking.

Seven gunmen hopped out on Andy with MP assault rifles circling him. Andy didn't have a gun on because he didn't ride around with guns and drugs; that was federal time.

Andy placed his hands in the air while they grabbed him, bringing him towards the open van.

Tat-tat-tat-tat-tat-tat-tat-tat-tat-tat-tat-tat-tat!

A gunman popped out from behind a garbage can, airing out the kidnappers and catching them off guard.

Andy saw the gunman's face and was shocked before he took off to his Benz. The seven shooters all laid on the ground dead. Wolf left through a backyard, taking shortcuts until he made it to his parked car. He tossed his AK-47 in the backseat and headed back to his crib with his first mission completed from Bella's father.

Aguilera wanted him to kill two of MS-13 niggas who were selling drugs and Crazy was next. Wolf had been tailing Dodge for days and tonight was perfect because Dodge was on his own mission to bring Andy to Crazy. When Wolf saw Dodge and his goons hop out on Andy, he made his move. He wondered why they wanted him.

Chapter 21

Washington Heights, NY

"You think he's coming here, bro? How did you even get the drop on this nigga so quickly?" Smurf started looking at the tall sky-rise building in front of them.

"The first time I saw this nigga I knew he was money, so I followed him. He must have a BM on the fifth floor because he always comes out with a bad Dominican bitch and a little infant." Andy said sitting behind the wheel of the new Tahoe RST SUV.

"You only re-upped from him once. I think we should at least get shit from him a couple more times before we book him, son," Smurf said, making sense.

"I can just save it and book him. Kill two birds with one bullet, bro," Andy said.

"A'ight. What happened the other night? I heard they found seven dead MS-13 niggas on Avon."

"Yeah, I tried to tell you in code, but it sounded like you were in a club. Them niggas tried to get me, bro. They hoped out on me with some big shit trying to toss me in a van"

"Word son," Smurf said, hyped up.

"Facts, bro, then the craziest happens."

"What?"

"You know Wolf?"

"Nah, who the fuck is that?" Smurf asked, knowing everybody in Yonkers.

"You remember the young basketball chick who Champ killed? Remember I was telling you that I shot at them niggas at the high school while you were gone?"

"I remember you telling me and you talking little Victoria from Elm. She's CB and Black's sister," Smurf said knowing who she was.

"Yeah, they got a little brother named Wolf. He a college kid. He lived up the block forever. He be pushing a black BMW, just a quiet kid," Andy said.

"I don't think I know him, but what about him? CB's name is heavy up north. He the big homie."

"He popped out with an AK and a drum, shooting like a madman. He almost hit me, bro, but he killed all them niggas. We made eye contact, bro, and the look in his eyes was cold."

"So, a college kid turned into a cold-blooded killer?" Smurf couldn't stop laughing because he knew Andy could be extra at times.

"Nigga deadass, son saved my life."

"That's Flaco…" Smurf said, focusing his attention on Flaco creeping into his baby mother's building by himself with a gym bag.

"It's too late to be coming from a gym," Andy said, cocking his gun. "Stick to the plan." Andy got out and followed Flaco into his baby mother's crib.

***

Flaco came from the Bronx picking up some money his workers owed him. He had plans to slide out to Queens after he placed the money in his safe.

This was one of four baby mothers he had, Flaco was a young pretty boy with a thing for bad bitches.

He walked into his crib in a rush to see Natti sitting in the living room feeding their six-week old infant.

"Papi, are you staying? I want to spend time with you tonight," Natti said, sitting on the couch in a silk robe and completely naked up under.

Natti was a beautiful Dominican woman, brown skin, long flat silky hair, thick curves, big titties, short, brown eyes, thick eyebrows, a small waist, thick glossy lips, and a perfect smile.

"I'm sorry, ma. I gotta go handle some business across town, then I gotta head out to Queens," he said, walking to the back room. He heard her curse and yell at him, but he paid her no mind. Flaco opened his safe in his closet which was already open because he never locked it. There was no need. If he couldn't trust his own BM, then who could he trust.

Flaco switched shoes into his Christian Louboutin to match his Balmain outfit, Cuban link chain, and bust down Rolex watch.

He was glad to hear Natti finally shut up because normally she would go non-stop. There were times where she would be yelling out the window and throwing shit at him when he left.

"Don't move," Smurf said, training his gun on Flaco rushing in on him while Andy had Natti at gunpoint with her infant in her hand.

"Andy, come on papa. You violate a bond like this? I did good to you, Papi," Flaco said, watching Natti cry. Smurf took Flaco's gun out of his back waistline and forced him into the living room.

"Where's the money and drugs, Flaco? Don't make this hard, bro please," Andy said.

"What money? It's nothing here. Let me make a call and I can get you whatever you want. Papi, you know I got it, just one call."

"Nigga, do I look dumb or stupid?" Andy said, getting upset and taking the baby out of Natti's hands.

"Nooooo!" Natti screamed.

"Shut up, bitch," Smurf yelled because he hated when people cried in pity.

"Flaco talk," Andy said with the infant in his arms, rocking him.

"Please let him go. All I need is to make a call. You can listen to it. I will have everything you need," Flaco said.

"Okay, have it your way, boy boy," Andy said, looking behind him to see a big microwave. Andy placed the baby inside the microwave and turned it on.

"Pleaseeeee!" Flaco cried with tears.

"Flacoooo tell them!" Natti yelled, seeing sparks go off in the microwave.

"Okay, it's in the room," Flaco said as Andy stopped the microwave to hear the baby cries and the burn spot on his face.

Smurf went into the room hunting for money and drugs to only come out seconds later with two bags of money.

"There is no drugs, only money," Smurf said looking at Andy.

Boc! Boc! Boc! Boc!

Andy fired slugs into Natti's head.

"You still want to play these games," Andy said, pointing the gun to the baby's head.

"It's in the closet by the front door under the floor, man," Flaco said, looking at Natti's dead body slumped on the couch.

Smurf went into the closet to see a rug on the floor, but when he removed the rug, he saw a loose piece of wood and removed it. After moving half the floor in the closet, he saw stacks of heroin.

"Jackpot, son," Smurf said, grabbing two heavy duffle bags from over his head loading them up.

"Can I have my son back? Y'all got what y'all came for, papa," Flaco said before Andy fired two shots into his face.

"Fuck outta here, son," Andy said to himself still holding the crying baby in his arms.

"Time to go," Smurf said, carrying a gang of bags and needing help.

"What should we do with this little nigga?"

"No witnesses, nigga," Smurf said.

"A'ight," Andy said, placing the infant back in the microwave for ten minutes before leaving the apartment with their hands full of bags.

"Baby killer," Smurf said laughing as they pulled off on their way back to Yonkers.

"Whatever nigga," Andy said, turning up the LOX's new album.

Chapter 22

Connecticut

"We have to be quick, in and out. If anybody moves, shoot them or they're going to shoot you. Be on point, son," Black said, driving the Hellcat on the Connecticut highway on his way to a local bank in Bridgeport, CT.

"So, we going in there on some *Set It Off* shit," Cap said from the backseat with a chopper in his lap.

"Nigga, you saw what happen to them bitches at the end of that movie?" Wisdom said looking back.

"Yeah," Cap replied.

"A'ight then clown ass nigga. We are going to stick to the plan. Me and you take out the three security guards, while Black is going to hop over the counter and get the money," Wisdom said in his deep voice like he was the mastermind.

Black recently met Cap and Wisdom in the Bronx at a lounge and they were telling him how they were robbing Western Unions all across the city. When Black brought up the idea about robbing a bank, they were both in for it.

Wisdom is a five percenter on the run from a murder in Queens, so he was living on the edge. Cap was his friend. He was a little slow, but he was a good nigga and down for whatever Wisdom had in mind.

"Stick to that plan. Just cover each other. At noon exactly, the Brinks truck picks up the money. So, at 11:40 am the cash will be in money bags on the floor, packed up and ready to go. It's going to be like taking candy from a baby," Black said, pulling off Exit 9 onto Bridgepoint's main streets.

"It's litty. I'm ready to smoke these niggas, burn their asses up, bust a cap in their ass. I'ma fuck these niggas raw like how I use to do in prison behind the wall," Cap shouted getting pumped up.

"What nigga?" Wisdom asked looking at Cap like he lost his mind, but he knew his friend wasn't wrapped to tight up top.

"This is it. I'ma go in first, twenty seconds later y'all come in and do y'all thing," Black said parking down the block.

"A'ight son, be safe," Wisdom said before Black hopped out with a hoodie on and sunglasses with a fake beard attached to his face for disguise.

Black walked into the cold bank to see three out of shape security guards eating donuts and drinking coffee as if they were real cops.

When Black was walking to the bank teller, all hell broke loose when Wisdom and Cap busted in the bank. Following them, shots could be heard.

Black saw both men shooting the security guards. He hopped over the counter to see three bags full of crispy money. He opened all of the bags checking for dye bombs to blow up, but all he found was two GPS systems.

Black tossed the small GPS system out of the bags and ran towards the door jumping over civilians' bodies that were lying on the floor and taking cover. Black saw the three guards with bullets all in the face, neck, and upper and lower torso. It was a gruesome sight.

Wisdom and Cap followed Black out of the door, racing off down the block. They pulled off in the Hellcat hearing sirens from a distance, but the Hellcat was already out of sight.

"Wipe them choppers down. We're about to toss them shits," Black said, pulling over on an old empty bridge.

"Do we have to?" Cap said sadly.

"Hell, yeah! What if we get pulled over?"

"Facts," Wisdom said, wiping down his chopper with his t-shirt. Everybody got out and they both tossed their murder weapon into the river.

"Good job," Black said, pulling out his pistol.

Boc! Boc! Boc! Boc! Boc! Boc!

Black gave both men three headshots a piece, then he flipped their bodies into the river.

Black hopped back into his Hellcat on his way back home from a long day of easy work. Black didn't trust either one of them. He planned this whole scene out from the first time he laid eyes on both of them.

***

Yonkers, NY

"This going to be a hot summer boy, I'm telling you. I'm trying to cop a Benz or a Jag," Dice said while he was posted on Cliff Street with a couple of his goons. Dice was selling dope for Andy and Smurf; he grew up with them. Cliff Street was up the block from Elm Street; it was connected.

"We're going to Summer Jam this weekend. I heard Meek Mill, Fab, 22oz, and Pop Smoke were going hit the stage," Fearsome said

"They killed son, I think," Pipe replied.

"Who?" Dice inquired, sipping lean in front of his building.

"Pop Smoke," Pipe said, rolling up a dub of exotic weed in a Dutch Masters.

"Yo, look at this drunk ass nigga, he on the wrong side of town," Dice said watching the drunk Mexican stumble up the block.

"Ain't no bars over here. Where he even come from? I hate them wetbacks," Pipe said.

"Let's show him how we do niggas out of band," Fearsome said, getting up from the building's stairs to beat up the Mexican.

When they got ten feet within the drunk man, a car parked in the middle of the block and three Mexicans popped out.

Bloc! Bloc! Bloc! Bloc!

Boom! Boom! Boom!

Dice shot one of the Mexicans, killing him. The drunk Mexican gave him two headshots and killed Pipe, who tried to run in a building, yet he hawked him down.

The Mexicans left all of them dead before going back across town to celebrate and drink Tequila.

***

Brooklyn, NY

Andy and Smurf were driving back to Yonkers from chilling with Tom Dog, a nigga Smurf did time with up top. He plugged them into some niggas who needed a good price on the keys. Smurf was on the phone apologizing to someone non-stop and telling them that he would handle it before hanging up.

"What happened?" Andy said, knowing something was wrong.

"Mexicans killed Dice and his crew," Smurf said.

"It's lit now, but we gotta pay Chopper a visit," Andy said, knowing someone was going to pay for his friend's death.

Chapter 23

Southside Yonkers
Days Later

Chopper only came out at nighttime and he would only walk to the store and back home to take care of his sick grandma.

The other day he saw Andy people topped off on a crime scene with white sheets everywhere but when he heard the police say something about a dead Mexican, he knew the city was about to get crazy.

Chopper fucked with Andy heavy. However, when he didn't pay him from the Ortiz lick, he wanted to see blood. Going to Crazy was his only choice and he needed money. Selling drugs was never his thing, he was more of a robber. Yet he only robbed gas stations for fast money.

The 24-hour Open store was on his block. He went in to grab a few things. After he brought a pack of Newport and a six pack of beer, he sent a text to a few women to see if they were free to chill. Chopper made his way back to his building so he could sniff some coke and call over a chick.

He saw his front door open and he always closed his door because his grandma was always inside. He walked inside to see nothing, which made him realize he must have left the door open.

"Think you fucking slick, nigga," Andy said from behind the door, pointing his gun to the back of Chopper's head. Andy lifted Chopper's long shirt and took his weapon.

"Andy, I can explain. Please, this is a big misunderstanding," Chopper tried to explain.

Whack!

Andy slapped him in the head with his pistol, knocking him on the floor.

"Smurf!" Andy yelled to see Smurf come out from the back with Chopper's grandma and grab her by her thin gray hair.

"Who did you tell Chopper? You better save her life," Andy said seriously, pointing his gun at his grandma.

"I'll tell you everything, just don't harm her. She old, man," Chopper said with mercy.

"Talk then, nigga. I don't have all day," Andy said.

"When you ain't pay me, I went to Crazy to tell him what you did to his brother, Ortiz."

"That's the MS leader, right?" Smurf asked. He had heard his name many times in jail.

"Somewhat, but the real big homie is Jimenez. He's their uncle and he's a Blackhand from Cali. He lives in L.I., but he be out here," Chopper said.

"You gave him my location?" Andy asked.

"No just where you be at on Elm Street. That's all, fool. I swear."

"Where can I find this Crazy nigga at?"

"You can't. He'll find you. He moves around so much it's hard to keep up," Chopper said.

Andy gave Smurf a head nod and Smurf blew his grandma's head off.

"Your turn," Andy said, forcing his gun into his mouth.

"I know his little sister. I used to fuck her. That's how I knew about Ortiz and Crazy," he cried, looking at his grandma die with her eyes wide open.

"Where can I find her?" Andy said.

"She works at a bar in White Plains called Thirsty Lounge. It's a Mexican bar, but she's a party girl, very wild and down for a good time. Mayte is a very beautiful girl, you won't miss her," Chopper said.

BOOM! BOOM! BOOM!

Blood squirted on Andy's Rag and Bone jeans and Timbs that he'd just brought.

"Damn, nigga! Who wears new Timbs on a mission?" Smurf said, laughing leaving. Smurf grabbed Chopper's cell phone.

"You want to go handle this?" Andy asked.

"Nah, let Dice's little bro, Force, and Lil Tom handle that shit. Let's find Crazy or some of his people," Smurf said, ready to put in some work.

Before the end of the night, eight Mexican gang members were found dead all around Yonkers thanks to Andy and Smurf.

***

White Plains, NY

Mayte's shift was ending in five minutes and she was going to a hotel party someone just texted her about and she wasn't going to miss it.

She was a college girl and part-time bartender at Thirsty Lounge on the weekend. She loved to go out and party with her friends or alone it didn't matter to her. Mayte was a full-blooded Mexican. She was tall, long legs, slim, flat ass, but she had a beautiful and alluring face.

Her family was all gangbangers. She didn't agree with their lifestyle, so she stayed away for the most part. However, the loss of her favorite brother, Ortiz, crushed her.

It was time for her to leave. The bar was slow tonight anyway, so she was not missing too much money or tips.

She got her belongings and walked to her Subaru Legacy. She played her favorite song by Lupita Infante called "Ya ni me acuerdo."

When she made it to the Marriott hotel which was close to her job, she popped some molly she had in her purse to get her in the mood. She was going to call her homegirls to come but she decided to wait until she figured out how lit the party was. She got changed in her car into a mini skirt and heel she had in the backseat she always kept just in case.

Mayte checked the text to see what room the party was going down at. She went to room 5B and knocked, but she wondered why there was no music playing. Seconds later a young cute black dude answer the door smoking a blunt

"Is this the party?" she asked.

"Yeah, we about to start. Come in," Force said, letting her inside the room full of smoke clouds, making her cough.

"It's starting a little late, Papi," she said sitting her purse down on the living room table.

"You can come in the back until everybody comes."

"Okay," she said, following him to the back room. When Force opened the door, she saw close to twenty young niggas with guns smoking and drinking, staring at her cheesing." I think I'll pass. I have to go," she said, trying to turn to leave. She couldn't get far because Force grabbed her, ripping off her clothes and raping her for over four hours until her pussy smelled like bloody fish. When they were done violating her, Force thought about his brother, Dice. Those memories were foremost on his mind as he pumped sixteen shots into her body at point-blank range.

Chapter 24

Southside Yonkers

Crazy just got a call from his cousin informing him that Mayte's body was found dead in a White Plains hotel. When Crazy heard her cry, he knew something was wrong.

He and Mayte had a hard sister and brother relationship, but he still loved her very much with all his heart. She was a good kid, focused on college, and her independence as a woman, so he let her live her young life. Crazy knew her death was because of his beef. He felt it, but she didn't deserve to die at nineteen years old. Crazy was in his closed bar calling his uncle and letting him know what happened to Mayte, trying his best to hold on to his tears.

After the phone call to his uncle, he had plans to go see his sister's body to confirm it was her, and then his uncle wanted him to come to Long Island.

Crazy left his small personal office to see his four goons dressed in baggy clothes and covered in MS-13 tattoos. Most of them were fresh from a small city called Sonsonate in El Salvador.

"Rovira, we have a problem. I want you to call all our homies in Brooklyn, the Bronx, Queens, and Long Island. Tell them to meet us out here first thing in the morning. We're going to settle this shit once and for all," Crazy said to his top general, Rovira, who was 6'7" and very aggressive.

"Si," Rovira said, reassuring him it will be done.

"We have to go," Crazy said, rushing out the bar so that they could look at his sister's deceased body.

Once outside, a white Yukon truck awaited them.

"Shit, I forgot to lock the safe," Crazy said, turning around on the dark street. He started to run back inside to lock the safe because he had keys of coke and heroin in there.

Crazy wasn't big on selling dope, but since Ortiz was dead, he had to pick up the slack because his uncle got bricks by the boatload. Inside, Crazy locked his safe and left locking up the bar he owned for three years now on a quiet Yonkers block.

Crazy turned around to see the Yukon truck's doors open with two dead bodies inside and two dead bodies a couple of feet away from him. He pulled out his gun looking up and down the dark block with four dim street lights trying to find the shooter who killed his men.

Psst! Psst!

Crazy felt his kneecaps go out. When he hit the floor, his gun fell on the curb.

"Ahhhhhhh!" Crazy screamed in pain, trying to move his legs looking around. He was able to see a shadow crossing the street with a military assault rifle.

When Crazy saw the man's face, he was confused because he never saw his face a day in his life.

"Andy sent you? Ahhhhhh!" Crazy asked in pain, trying to stop the blood leaking out his legs.

"No," Wolf said before firing two shots into his forehead and then walking off in a calm demeanor.

Crazy was the other target on Aguilera's hit list. Wolf had been watching the bar for three weeks now. Tonight, he told himself he was going to strike, and he did just that. He wondered what he wanted with Andy or what they had going on.

Wolf had been so busy that he forgot to pull up on Andy for trying to save his life. Wolf never said a word to Andy or most niggas from Elm Street.

***

The Next Night

Wolf was coming from his mom's house, heading home so he could eat the dinner that Bella had cooked. Her cooking skills were the best. The girl could have been a chef.

It was raining heavily outside, but it was supposed to be a rainy week. Wolf had been so lousy he hadn't been keeping tabs on Champ, but he knew he was somewhere lurking and looking for answers to his family's death. Wolf wanted him to see how it felt to lose a loved one and then he planned to kill him.

Wolf had been trying his best to keep his new life away from Bella, but it was hard because she recently moved in with him. She wasn't only a cop in the streets, but at home also. She would sometimes go through his phone pockets, smell his underclothes, smell his scent to see if it changed. Wolf was overwhelmed, but he really loved her; she was a wonderful woman.

Pulling onto his street, he saw flashing lights behind him, which made him pull over. He had nothing in the car, so he was good. He followed all the traffic signs, so he didn't understand what was going on.

Wolf saw two undercover detectives hop out of the Crown Vic. Both men were familiar, he saw them many times and knew who they were. *Beavis and Butthead.*

"Pull your window, little nigga," Officer Steel said as Wolf rolled his window down.

"Good afternoon, officer. How may I help you?" Wolf said respectful with his hands on the wheel and not making any movement because police brutality was at an all-time high across the world. A young black man died at the hands of the police every day.

"Cut the small talk. What's a young kid like you doing a new BMW?" Steels asked.

"Yeah, where are the drugs at?" Sanderson asked, looking into the windows of the car with his flashlight.

"Sir, I…" Wolf said before he was cut off.

"Did I tell you to talk? Get the fuck out of the car now!" Steels shouted, drawing his gun on Wolf. Without arguing, Wolf got out with his hands in the air until Sanderson tossed him on the hood of the BMW and searched him.

Steels searched the car real quick to find nothing, getting upset, plus it was raining on him.

"He's a college kid," Sanderson said looking at his college ID.

"He's clean," Steel said, lifting Wolf off the hood.

"Why are y'all harassing me? Because I'm black or Spanish?" Wolf said upset. Both cops looked at each and laughed. They started beating the shit out of Wolf. They were hitting him with the flashlight and stomping on him until he was lying in a small puddle of blood.

When they were done, they climbed in the work car, pulling off to see Bella running down the street. When she got to Wolf, he was breathing, but hurt bad. She got him inside the BMW and drove him to St. Joseph's Hospital down the street. Bella just so happened to look out her window waiting for Wolf to surprise him with dinner. To her surprise, she saw two white boys stomping him out and hitting him with big flashlights.

Inside the hospital, Wolf was seen quickly; the nurses and doctors brought him to the back where he was in stable condition.

"Mrs. Aguilera, hi. Your boyfriend is okay, just a little banged up. He took a bad beating with four broken ribs, twenty stitches and nothing else is really serious. You can go in and see him. He can leave tonight," the doctor said before walking off to another area of the hospital.

Bella walked into Wolf's room and couldn't help but cry while looking into his concupiscent eyes.

"It's okay, babe," he said in a low voice hard to talk.

"No, it's not okay!" she screamed in pain for him.

"I fell, shit happens."

"I saw what they did to you, Romeo. It's not right," she said, crying uncontrollably and holding his hand.

"Baby, let's go home and forget this ever happened. Help me up," Wolf said trying to get up wanting her to forget about what happened tonight.

"You're not going to report it? Romeo, you have to."

"I'm no snitch," he said, getting her upset because she didn't understand the snitching code. She helped him all the way back home pissed off.

Chapter 25

Hunts Point, Bronx

Officer Steels was off duty today and he was living in a cheap motel in a well-known drug infected and prostitution area. Last night, Steels and Sanderson robbed a local drug dealer for twenty pounds of weed, seventy keys of coke, and $140,000 in cash. Steels was holding everything in his hotel room, waiting until Sanderson came to get his cut later.

Driving around the block, he saw who he was looking for; a Black hooker who called herself Heather. She was dark skin, skinny, and cute with some good pussy and head.

"Hey, daddy. I see you back three times in one week. My asshole is still sore from two nights ago, you big freak," Heather said leaning inside his driver's side window. She wore a mini skirt, old busted heels, and a dirty yellow tank top.

"Sure, the strip is dead anyway. I already caught two dates, so I'm good. My pimp will be trippin on me if I don't bring back the daily perfect," she said, seriously.

"It's cool. I got you. I got coke for you and everything to get you right."

"Oh, how come you didn't say so? That's my type of party," she said getting inside the car.

"What do you do for a living, daddy? Because you don't look like the type to be out here looking for a whore," she asked, putting lip gloss on her thick lips.

"I'm a construction site owner and I'm going through a divorce, so coming out here is my getaway," he said, pulling into the hotel parking lot.

"I'm here to help you relieve yourself, daddy. All in my mouth and tight ass pussy," she said, rubbing his penis.

"I know. Let's go inside," Steels said, horny and ready to get the party started.

Inside, Steels gave her a whole ounce of coke and a pound of weed; she was overwhelmed.

"Oh my God! Are you a drug dealer?" she said, placing a line of coke on the glass and sniffing it. Instantly feeling the rush because it was good coke.

"Far from that," he said, stripping down to his boxers. He didn't do drugs. He had to take a monthly piss test because he was on the precinct's hotlist.

"Come here, daddy," she said standing up so he can sit in the room chair. Steels sat in the chair and Heather got on her knees pulling out his small penis playing with the head with her tongue.

"Mmmmm," he moaned while she wrapped her lips around his dick coming up and down while massaging his balls. She was giving him sloppy head.

"Suck that dick right," he moaned holding on to the armrest with his head leaned back on cloud nine. Her oral sex was so amazing, he wished he could just cut her head off and carry it around.

"I always wondered why cops took an oath they never kept," Wolf said, coming out the bathroom with a Glock 27 pointed at both of them.

Heather took cover on the floor, covering her head like a bomb was about to go off.

"You little bastard! I should have killed you," Steels said, looking at Wolf black and blue face.

"Should have, could have, would have, bitch!"

Boc! Boc! Boc! Boc!

Wolf killed Steels and Heather, executing them with headshots. Wolf was on his way out when he saw a police duffle bag on the floor. Bella carried one every day to work. He took the bag and then placed a ski mask over his face before leaving. Wolf had been waiting for this day for two weeks while on bedrest.

***

Elm St, Yonkers

Yesterday Wolf was driving through Elm St and his neighbor Peanut told him Andy was trying to get at him, so he gave Wolf Andy's number.

Wolf called Andy and they set up an early morning meeting at a small park in the cut on a dead-end block.

It was nine in the morning and Wolf had to go meet Bella pops at noon in Tarrytown. He sat on the park benches waiting for Andy. He saw a Benz pull up next to his BMW making his car look like shit.

"Wolf," Andy said, extending his hand.

"Andy," Wolf replied, shaking his hand.

"Man, who the fuck are you? A ninja," Andy said, making him laugh.

"Nah, I was just paying you back a favor."

"That wasn't a favor, bro. I went to school with Victoria. She was good peoples. She didn't deserve to die. Champ and I got some beef anyway."

"Oh?"

"Yeah, somebody murdered his family. That boy's sick," Andy said looking at Wolf for answers but saw none.

"Karma is a dangerous game," Wolf added.

"Facts bro, but you really saved my life. Thank you," Andy said, seriously and taking a seat next to him.

"I have no idea what you're talking about," Wolf said.

"I'm not wired or nothing, my nigga. I'ma jack boy. I got myself into a little situation, but you came through for me. I owe you, bro," Andy said.

"If I had a business proposal, would you accept it?"

"It depends what it is, bro. I'm all about making bread," Andy replied looking at his bruised face.

"Follow me."

"What happened to your face if you don't mind me asking?"

"Beavis and Butthead."

"Damn son, that's fucked up, but Karma is a bitch. I heard they found Steels dead in a hotel in the Bronx," Andy said, quickly putting two and two together. "You're a beast, son," Andy said, shocked.

"You got the wrong person."

"I know and I'm Michael Jackson," Andy said looking as Wolf popped the trunk of his car filled with drugs.

"Can you move this and give me 50%?"

"Yeah. How much do you want to sell it for?"

"You put a price on it," Wolf replied.

"Okay, I'll have the money for you later. Meet me here at 9:30 PM and you shouldn't be riding around dirty like this. You wilding, bro."

"I don't sell drugs, bro, but I will be having a lot soon and I need someone I can trust."

"How do you know you can trust me?" Andy asked.

"Because you saved my life and I saved yours. Quiet was kept," Wolf said.

"Facts," Andy said, grabbing the drugs out of his trunk and placing it inside his Benz. "You must be into some big shit, son. Just be safe; it's a cold game out here. True you got a mean shot, but snakes are always lurking."

"I'm well prepared for anything. I'll see you later," Wolf said, climbing in his car while Andy walked down the block.

"You need a ride? You left your car?" Wolf said, pulling up on Andy.

"Hell, nah. I ain't riding with you, crazy ass nigga. You might have a bomb in that bitch and my little homie coming to pick the Benz up. I'm hot out here. The police love fucking with me, my G," Andy said.

"A'ight," Wolf said, driving down the block. He began putting his plan together. Now he had someone to push drugs for him. He put the money he got from Steels in the safe he had at his mom's house.

Chapter 26

Tarrytown, NY

Aguilera sat outside of a coffee shop eating a bagel with cream cheese, drinking Colombian coffee, and reading the *Wall Street Journal*.

Aguilera had been keeping tabs on Wolf and he did his job correctly leaving no trace or mess. The police accused Crazy and Dodge's murders of a gang war across the city.

He saw Wolf walk through the small gate of the outside area of the coffee shop with a fucked-up face.

"Damn kid, who you owed money to Mike Tyson? Look like them cops fucked you with no Vaseline," Aguilera said laughing shaking his head.

"The mission is done. What do you want now?" Wolf said sitting down and not in a joking mood.

"Lighten up a little… You did a good with the MS-13, perfect timing."

"I don't have all day."

"Okay, there is a man named Christ Telford. He is a Wall Street Accountant in Manhattan. He is very rich and cocky. Trust me, he's a real asshole. He was my college roommate for three years, but I need you to handle him. This is his address," Aguilera said sliding him a small piece of paper with a Lower Eastside address on it.

"A'ight, I'll take care of it."

"Yes, you will. But on another note, I heard Bella moved in with you?"

"Yeah."

"Do you think Yonkers is a safe place to lay your head after killing the MS leaders and Officer Steels?" Aguilera said, as he continued to drink his coffee.

Wolf's facial expression said it all. He was confused, all he was thinking was how he knew about Steels. He made sure nobody followed him, he spun the block four times to make sure.

"No worries, I made sure everything was cleaned up. But back to the question," Aguilera asked.

"I'ma take care of it soon, but I don't need you to tell me how to live my life," he said standing.

"While you're in Bella's life that makes your life a part of mine," he said to Wolf's back as he walked out.

***

Yonkers, NY

Tonight, the Yonkers Police Department was planning to do a raid on an apartment building on Wartburg Street. They were looking for a fugitive on the run for a double homicide. The caller gave the police a tip on where SG was staying. The caller was his baby mother who was jealous he was fucking with a new bitch.

"The backup should arrive in ten minutes. You ready for your first raid?" Kingston asked his partner, Bella, who was on her phone texting.

"What happened?" she said paying him no mind because she didn't fuck with him at all. She only was his partner because her higher upper wouldn't reassign her partners yet. She would have to wait a year.

"Nothing," he said, taking a deep breath. They both wore plain clothes and were parked in an undercover car with tints so they wouldn't be spotted.

"Is that him?" Bella said seeing SG walk out the building with a bookbag in precipitance speed.

"We can't let him go," Kingston said, getting out of the car to pursue the wanted seventeen-year-old.

Bella had no choice but to follow Kingston as he ran across the street with his gun drawn.

"Freeze!" Kingston yelled

SG looked back to see two undercover cops a few feet away and he took off running up the hill.

Kinston and Bella chased him, but SG was fast. Kingston saw he was losing him and fired eight rounds, hitting SG in his back six times, and taking him down.

"Yesss!" Kingston shouted.

Bella couldn't believe what she just saw, she called it in on her walkie talkie.

"Shots fired, fugitive down!" she screamed in her radio approaching SG. When she saw the tears in his eyes, she couldn't help but cry for him.

"I can't breathe... help me please..." he said on his back, choking on his own blood.

"Hold on. It's okay," she said holding his hand and feeling his grip loosen up before his eyes rolled in the back of his head.

"You saw him reach for a gun, okay? That's our story" Kingston said pacing knowing he just fucked up again. Sirens could be heard closing in on them coming up the hill

"I'm not lying for you at all. You killed him for nothing. I'm not saying shit. Your body cam will tell the truth," she said standing up.

"Shit..." he yelled, forgetting he had his body cam on his vest.

When the police arrived, SG was long gone. Kingston told the sergeant on duty what happened, and he was suspended on the spot blaming Bella.

***

Yonkers, NY
Day Later

"Where are we going?" Bella said getting out of Wolf's car in front of the new condos near the waterfront which was the tourist and nice area of Yonkers.

"Shhh..."

"Don't tell me to shush... This place is nice. Who you know that lives here?" she asked Wolf, following him into the glass luxury building.

"You ask a lot of questions, babe."

"I know," she said in the elevator. They got off on the sixth-floor walking to the end of the hall. Wolf walked into the apartment with white marble floors throughout the condo, four bedrooms, three bathrooms, two walk-in closets, and 5,472 square feet.

"Wow this is fancy and beautiful," Bella said looking at the three-sided fireplace in the living room, a living room sunroof in the glass ceiling because they were on the highest level.

"You like it, babe?"

"Hell yeah!"

"Good. It's ours, paid in full. I leased it for a year."

"Oh my God! I love you so much," she said jumping into his muscular arm kissing him. Bella brought him over to the kitchen marble countertop and lifted her dress up showing no panties and her bald pretty ass pussy. Wolf pulled his dick out and fucked her like a pro all over the kitchen for over an hour and a half.

Chapter 27

Elm St, Yonkers

Sanderson sat in his Ford Taurus with tints watching low-level hustlers sell drugs to a thousand fiends coming from all over the city to get the best heroin for the lowest price.

Losing Steels was rough on him because someone stole the drugs and money, he had plans for. When he went to the hotel to pick up his half, he found Steels dead with a black hooker.

Sanderson searched the room to come up with nothing, so he knew it was a robbery. The murder was still unsolved, but Sanderson had a long list of people who could be responsible for his partner's death.

First on his list was Sheek, who just came home from a ten-year bid thanks to Steels putting drugs on him. Steels shot Sheek twice after Sheek knocked him out and woke him back up. The two hated each other, so Sheek was his main target.

***

Sheek walked out his baby mother's crib on Elm Street and Oak Street to see niggas trapping hard, remembering him of himself years ago. Sheek worked at Walmart and was focus on taking care of his family. He just came home from up north months ago and he left the streets alone because he feared going back to prison. Ten years took everything out of him, and he lost everything.

When Sheek came home everybody tried to give him drugs so he could get on his feet, but nobody tried to show him a better way. He refused the drugs and fake love his niggas gave him and focused on getting his life in order.

Sheek was a big boy standing at six feet and two hundred sixty-two pounds with a head full of long dreads that flowed down his back.

"My old friend, Sheek," Sanderson said, walking across the street towards Sheek who stopped at the sound of the familiar voice.

"What the fuck you want piece of shit?" Sheek said with a sour face. There were many nights when Sheek could dream of hurting Beavis and Butthead for fucking up his life.

"Welcome home. I heard you had a tough bid being a big Crip and everything. That's a nice scar on your face."

"Sorry to hear about your boyfriend. A dickhead like that didn't even deserve to make FOX News," Sheek said, seeing Sanderson's face turn red.

"Get on the car with your hands up!"

"What man? I ain't do shit," Sheek said.

"Get on the fucking car now." Sanderson pulled out his gun while civilians surrounded him.

"A'ight, calm down," Sheek said getting on the old model car next to him because he knew Sheek wouldn't hesitate to shoot a nigga.

Sanderson patted Sheek down roughly.

"You got a smart mouth, boy. I'ma fix that shit today, little nigga," Sanderson said.

"You wilding."

"You killed my partner, didn't you?"

"What nigga? I'm on house arrest. I can only go to work and church," Sheek said honestly before Sanderson body slammed Sheek on the floor as if he was a pro wrestler. Sanderson placed his knee on Sheek's neck and one in his back cutting off his oxygen supply.

"Stop resisting!" Sanderson yelled.

"I can't breathe," Sheek screamed over twenty times, unable to move or breathe.

"Stop talking then nigger," Sanderson stated.

"You're going to kill him," a young man in the crowd yelled videotaping this gruesome act.

Sanderson had his knee on Sheek's neck for eight minutes and forty-eight seconds, but Sheek was already dead at the seven minutes mark.

"He's dead!" someone yelled.

Sanderson felt no pulse on Sheek's neck and called it in. The crowd of civilians was crying and screaming because another black man's life was stolen at the hands of the police.

***

Long Island, NY

"You've been a help out here in Long Island, but we need you in Yonkers since we lost my two nephews," Jimenez told Alvarado, one of his best soldiers in New York.

"Okay, I have no problem with that. But do you know who we're at war with out there, so I can keep the homies on alert?" Alvarado asked.

"I have one name, Andy. To have killed both of my nephews, he must be a hell of a man,"

"Where is this Andy located?"

"Elm Street. A long uphill section full of blacks but all of our homies will be all over the Southside area," Jimenez stated, sitting in his large courtyard in the back of his mansion.

"Good to know, I will take care of them first"

"You have to be cautious these are not your regular wannabe thugs. You have to be very patient and prepared to deal with Andy and whoever he runs with because I see he's sharp," Jimenez said, strongly making eye contact with Alvarado letting him know they were the real deal.

"It will be handled, big homie."

"Good, but how's business going?"

"Fair. We've been dealing with the Puerto Ricans in Queens. They spend big money especially Mueto," Alvarado said.

"Mueto is a good man and good business," Jimenez said, looking into the beautiful sky.

"I'ma go and get everybody ready for the move to Yonkers"

"Yes, Pitbull is waiting for your call. He's been handling the drug trade, but he's not built for war and battle like you are."

"I understand. Have no worries, fool. I got you," Alvarado said, leaving.

Alvarado was a New Yorker from Long Island. He was an MS-13 gang member and a vicious killer. He controlled the Long Island and Queens area for his gang, and they had the murder at an all-time high. This crew kidnapped judges, drug lords, rival gangs, and tortured them leaving bodies all across Long Island and Queens.

Chapter 28

Lower Eastside, NY

Mr. Hatchmen was on his way to his 17.5-million-dollar condo from his Wall Street office where he owed his own accountant company called Hatch Accounting Cooperation. His company was worth billions and was one of the biggest account companies in the city.

His driver pulled his new 650 Maybach into the lower garage level of his condo overseeing the beautiful bright city.

Hatchmen grew up in Manhattan under a very rich family. His father was a hotel owner and his mother was a federal judge in Manhattan. He went to an Ivy League college to become one of the biggest accountants in New York.

He took the private elevator to the penthouse suite where he lived with his personal maid. She was a beautiful, young, and attractive French woman, whom he would have sexual intercourse with.

Marriage and kids weren't in his plans; he loved the single free life without being tied down, but he had so many different bitches he lost track of their names. He loved Spanish and white women. He was a very handsome white boy with swag and class.

Hatchmen got off his penthouse elevator stepping foot directly into his luxury condo to see darkness. He walked further into his condo and stopped.

"Would you like some tea or coffee?" Hatchmen said to the man he saw sitting in his living room chair.

"No thank you," Wolf said in a suit and tie with a pistol in his lap with a silencer on the barrel.

Hatchmen walked into the living to see his maid on the kitchen floor with bullet holes in her neck laying in a pool of blood.

"Let me guess. Aguilera sent you," Hatchmen said sitting down across from Wolf calm and at ease showing no signs of concern or fright.

"You must have seen this coming," Wolf stated in a tone of prowess

"Aguilera always wanted to be me. Rich, smart, powerless, and successful, but he just didn't make the cut."

"So, you two have a lot of history. I'm sure there is more than jealousy or envy."

"You must not know Aguilera," Hatchmen said honestly.

"Not I don't"

"He stole my college girlfriend and married her. He even gave her a beautiful daughter from what I hear. But while he was married, she was still having an affair with me. She was truly in love with me and he couldn't let that go. You see, Romeo, a tender dick person is the worst kind of person you want to deal with because they will cross whoever to fulfill their own emotional pleasures," said Hatchmen in his soft proper business-like tone.

"How do you know my name?" Wolf asked.

"I know a lot, Wolf. Money can get you a lot of things in life, but I'm willing to face death. I lived an amazing life. I've been waiting for you to arrive, but you have a lot of potential. Don't let Aguilera suck you dry and flush you. Outsmart him at his own game or you will only be a pawn on his chessboard," Hatchmen stated seriously, looking him in his eyes.

"Thanks for the encouragement and good words, but I have to get going," Wolf said.

"Guess I'll see you around."

"Bye."

PSST! PSST! PSST! PSST! PSST! PSST!

Hatchmen's body vibrated with bullets, sending him into a shock before he died.

Wolf made his exit thinking about his whole conversation with Hatchmen and how Aguilera wanted his head because he was fucking his wife. Wolf felt like shit for murdering a man over a bitch, and a dead bitch at that.

***

Queens, NY

The club was packed playing the hottest Reggaeton music in the city. Major artists came through to perform and promote their music. Daddy Yankee and Bad Bunny were two of the club regulars because they knew Mueto, the club owner from Puerto Rico.

Mueto was a club owner in Queens and he owned three big clubs in Puerto Rico where he was born and raised. He was raised in a small town called Arroyo, Puerto Rico with a poor family in poverty.

When he came to New York, his life changed. He met a plug and never looked back. Once he got in position to give back, he opened clubs in Puerto Rico that were now a success.

He used to re-up from Ortiz but now he was dealing with Alvarado and business was better than ever.

Mueto was dark-skinned and most confused him with being African American, but he was full-blooded Puerto Rican. He was waiting on his guest to arrive for a meeting about drug prices on his keys.

His office was on the basement level of the club. He kept two guards outside his door and two more upstairs watching the club partygoers because sometimes civilians got drunk and acted crazy.

"Boss, they're here."

"Let them in," Mueto said sitting behind an oakwood desk with keys everywhere. One of his clients named Rico P told him about two young hustlers looking for big weight and he sent them to him. Mueto didn't really fuck with too many people because everybody was ratting these days, so he kept his circle tight.

"Gentlemen have a seat," Mueto said, looking at both young men sit down across from him looking into their eyes feeling them out.

"I'm Andy and this is my brother, Smurf. Thanks for meeting with us. To get straight to the point, we need a new plug. We're from Yonkers and we got money upfront, so we don't want nothing on the arm," Andy said.

"Slow down, Papi... I like your style and attention, but let's take it one step at a time."

"I agree," Smurf said.

"So, who was y'all last connect?" Mueto asked because he knew every plug in New York.

"Flaco," Andy said.

"Young Flaco he was a good kid. I liked him a lot. That was sick what happened to his family. Someone killed his baby in a microwave. I was surprised because I never heard anything like that before," Mueto said getting cold chills thinking about his seven kids.

"I was saddened also," Andy said.

"His sister took over now and she is a crazy bitch, but sexy. Anyway, how much weight y'all plan to cop daily?" Mueto asked.

When he said those words, Andy and Smurf looked at each other and pulled out guns.

Boc! Boc! Boc!

Smurf shot Mueto in his eyes, killing him. His two guards rushed in with their guns drawn, but Andy's bullets penetrated their hearts, knocking them down. Smurf grabbed the bags near the open safe full of money and took all the bricks off the table. He was sure to also grab the money out of the safe while Andy held down the door.

When everything was bagged up, they made their way through the packed club out the back unnoticed.

Chapter 29

Greenburg, NY

Wolf pulled into the diner to meet Aguilera again to inform him about Hatchmen's death. Things at home were great. Living with Bella was marvelous. She was the perfect woman and sexy. He was in his own world.

He planned to get a new car tomorrow, not only for himself but for Bella's birthday also. The money Andy paid him came in handy. He liked Andy. He was loyal and humble. Andy told him about his boy, Smurf, who he has yet to meet. Andy planned to introduce the two soon because they were all on the same team.

The agreement he had with Aguilera was really starting to take a toll on him, but there was no way around it. Truth be told, Wolf was starting to look forward to killing niggas and reaping the financial benefits.

Inside the diner, he saw Aguilera drinking a glass of water and sitting in front of two plates full of breakfast food at 11:30 PM.

Bella wanted to know where he was going this late, but he told her to his mom's house. He didn't like lying to her, but he had no choice because Bella wasn't only Aguilera's daughter, but she was still a cop and he didn't trust her a hundred percent.

"Good afternoon," Aguilera said looking at him up and down checking out the new designer attire he saw all the young people wearing.

"This is for me?" Wolf said pointing at the plate.

"Yes, please eat with me," Aguilera said, cutting his sausages and pancakes with his eye trained on him.

"You called me all the way out here for a dinner date? I could have been in the bed with your daughter or in her guts," Wolf said with a smirk, making Aguilera stop eating.

"You watch your damn mouth, you little piece of shit," Aguilera said, banging his fist on the table.

"Get your thongs out your ass. Who's next so I can get the fuck out of here?" Wolf asked.

Aguilera slid him a brown envelope under the table. "Don't look at it now, too many eyes."

"It's five people in here."

"You never know who's who," Aguilera said, looking around.

"Facts, but Hatchmen told me that he was banging your wife or some shit. I never saw anyone so at peace before they died," Wolf said looking at Aguilera's tense face.

"This meeting is over," Aguilera said, suddenly rushing to get up to leave.

Wolf finished his meal because he was starving and laughing to himself for finally hitting a nerve on him.

***

School Street, Yonkers

Lil Tom was in School Street Projects Building 77 with his girlfriend trying his best to calm her down. He'd been fucking with Jada since he was fourteen years old, they knew each other better than anybody.

"Lil Tom, you have been in my fucking crib fucking me all night raw and shit, playing with my emotions and you in this bitch sneak texting other bitches!" Jada yelled waking him up out of his sleep.

Jada was a pretty tall brown skin diva, slim, long micro braids, big titties, hazel eyes, a nice round ass, and some grade one pussy, but she was crazy.

The couple had been fucking all night. She put him to sleep, but she was laying down fake sleep waiting for him to knock out so she can break through his password and invade his privacy. When she saw he was texting six different women, she was hurt.

Since he copped a Benz and a Rolex watch, she saw how much he changed since he was getting money.

"Jada give me my phone. You wilding, ma. Them hoes ain't about shit. You're number one. You know I love you," he said kissing her neck while she tried to push herself away.

"No, nigga! Fuck outta here! You're not going to butter me up tonight. Get the fuck out!" she shouted hopping out the bed in her bra and thongs as her ass giggled and clapped every time she moved.

"What Jada? It's 2:15 AM. You tripping. Lay down. I'ma delete all these bitches' numbers," he said.

"Too late. You can keep them hoes. I'm sick of your shit! That's why I've been fucking your friend, Arty, and his dick is snapping! Now get the fuck out!" she yelled with tears crossing her arms over her chest.

Lil Tom was shocked she would violate like that; he had a feeling something was wrong with Arty because every time he called him, Arty would hang up on him.

"You dirty bitch," Lil Tom said, getting dressed in his skinny jeans placing his 380-special gun in his back pocket.

"That's why Arty got herpes, bitch," Lil Tom said leaving.

"Well, if I got it, you got it nigga!" she yelled behind him, slamming her apartment door. Lil Tom put on his iPhone headphones to listen to the new A Boogie wit da Hoodie album.

Lil Tom walked to the elevator, but it was broken as always. He went to the staircase to smell piss and see spray paint everywhere saying Trap Stairs, Ruff Ryders, and D-Block.

Lil Tom turned the corner on the sixth flight in the dim stairwell to be attacked by two Mexicans with big, sharp, long knives.

The Mexicans pinned him to the wall stabbing him no-stop sixty-four times, killing him.

Alvarado opened the sixth-floor stairwell door to see Lil Tom slumped on the floor bleeding all over the place making him smile before walking off with his two soldiers.

They'd been waiting on Lil Tom for hours. They even broke the elevator so they could catch Lil Tom in the dark staircase. Luckily, the old building had no cameras, so they wore no masks.

Alvarado knew at this time nobody would be out, so it was perfect. Alvarado did his full research on Andy and his crew. It only took days to figure out Lil Tom was someone close to him, so he aimed for him first.

Romell Tukes

Chapter 30

Southside, Yonkers

"All these Mexican gangs look-alike, bro. How can we tell the difference?" Smurf asked Andy.

"Nigga, they all stay on their own turf with each gang having their own street, dummy. Now strap up," Andy said hiding on the floor under a pick-up truck with Smurf who was talking too much.

They had been there over twenty minutes watching the Mexicans in the alley smoke and drink in the back of a baby shower.

The night Lil Tom was killed in the School Street Projects, a couple of niggas said they saw some Mexicans leaving the building. When Andy heard this, he knew it was a direct hit. He thought with Ortiz and Crazy dead the beef would die down, but it was only about to get worse.

Lil Tom's death sparked a heatwave across the city everybody loved Lil Tom. His brother, Trigger, was in Yonkers looking for answers and he had $150,000 for anyone that could point him in the direction of his killers.

"Let's get this shit over with bro," Andy said, cocking his Draco assault rifle then rolling himself from under the truck with Smurf following his lead.

They ducked low while sneaking up on the crew of MS-13 gangsters drinking in broad daylight at one of their sisters' baby shower. They were all in the backyard opening gifts with family members enjoying the evening.

Tat, tat, tat, tat, tat, tat, tat, tat, tat...

Smurf and Andy cleared the alley and then started into the back yard as people ran all over the place, taking cover from the hail of bullets.

The chick whose baby shower it was laid on the floor with four bullets to her large pregnant stomach, taking her last breath.

Andy and Smurf saw over ten dead bodies and ran down the alley to their getaway car.

***

Auburn Maximum-Security Prison

"Where Two Gunz go this morning, skrap?" CB asked his homie, Yellow, from Albany, New York.

"Son went to court, bro. I think he about to give some time back," Yellow said, leaning on his cell bars about to go to the Education Building to get his GED.

"Damn, I thought that was next month, bro."

"Me too. I guess they got blood early," Yellow said, walking off while OG walked down the tier nodding his head at a couple of the young cats from Brooklyn that he had a small liking for.

"Yellow, what's good, young blood?" OG said, walking in his cell.

"Ain't shit, OG. I'm about to go take this GED test."

"Good luck!" OG shouted to Yellow who was halfway down the long tier which held eighty-four cells. There were three levels on each block, A-D.

"What's up OG Chuck? Where you been?" CB said, walking into OG's clean cell with prayer rugs and stacks of Islamic books everywhere.

"I was outside getting early morning money in the weight shack. Morning time is the best time to get your blood flowing, plus it gives you peace of mind," OG said, getting his hygiene ready for the shower.

"Facts. Did you speak to Major and Loon?"

"Yeah, Loon said his people sent you $10,000 and Major said he needs another month or so because he accidentally flushed the pack while taking a shit," OG said, laughing knowing that was bullshit.

"The little homie playing games like that? A'ight."

"You know how it goes, youngsta," OG said.

"Mr. Jackson, cell 224, you have a visit!" a C.O. yelled on the intercom.

"I gotta get ready. I wasn't expecting anybody today," CB said.

"It may be one of them chicks from the dating sites you be on. I forgot to tell you. I got a new hit on *Write-a-prison*.com. She's a fat white chick, but she pays like she weighs, so that's all that matters. I'll be on the dance floor soon," OG said, walking to the shower down the hall.

***

CB walked into the visiting room to see no familiar face until he looked near the window. He couldn't believe who it was.

"CB, what's up?" Wolf said seeing how huge his older brother got.

"What's poppin', bro? You looking like a grown man," CB said, sitting down glad to see Wolf.

"Yeah, time be moving."

"Facts. Congratulations on your degree, bro. We need more young black brothers like you out there. I'm proud of you," CB said from his heart.

"Thanks. I'm just trying to help my people because this shit is a trap off top. It was designed to hurt us as a whole."

"True, it's been a while," CB said.

"Five years was the last time I saw you, but you were in Attica I believe

"Yeah, you and mommy pulled up to see me before I went to the box," CB stated.

"How you holding up in there?"

"I take it one day at a time. Boy, shit be so brazy because only the strong survive in here and the weak will be destroyed. This shit will test your manhood every day and you have to put on a show. Any moment of weakness and you become Lion meat."

"Damn, this sounds like the streets."

"Worst nigga, that's why I'm glad you live a square life," CB added.

"Yeah, I got a little badass Puerto Rican chick. She's a cop," Wolf said.

"Okay, you better put a seed in that nigga because bitches ain't shit. But when you get a good girl, you better hold on tight to her, son," CB said.

"You right, bro. Bitches be trying to holla at me all day, but they not on shit," Wolf said.

"Fuck 'em. Don't risk what you got for nothing worse or less. What's good with Black?"

"I don't know, to be honest."

"Yeah, all he wants to do is rob banks," CB said already knowing how Black moved.

The visit lasted two more hours, but Wolf promised to come back again soon when the time was right. He had a lot going on, he disclosed.

Chapter 31

Long Island, NY

"How do you even know about this nigga and his family?" Smurf asked, tailing an Audi truck on the highway.

"Why the fuck you ask so many questions, bro?" Andy said, keeping tabs on the truck.

"I gotta know where we going and what we doing. It's only right, my G," Smurf replied pushing the gas on the Mustang. He was swerving through traffic trying not to lose the Audi.

"I know people that know people. Is that good enough for you?"

"Don't ask me to come on no more missions," Smurf said, getting aggravated with Andy's full attention.

"That sounds like music to my ears. I didn't ask you to come on this one or the last one. You just want some smoke, nigga, you can't help it," Andy said knowing Smurf better than himself.

"You think you got me figured out, huh? Fuck outta here, nigga. I gave my life to the Lord last week, bro. We have been sinning too much."

"What nigga? Who baptized you, Charles Mason?" Andy said, laughing so hard he had tears.

"You gotta change one day, bro."

"You right, but today won't be the day. Plus, I want to try this new shit out," Andy said, pulling out a small box with a beeping red light from a book bag.

"What the fuck is that?" Smurf said following the Audi truck off an exit.

"An explosive I brought from a Muslim in the Bronx last week," he said. He made it himself.

"That shit comes with instructions?" Smurf asked with a fearful look in his eyes.

"Nah, son told me to place it somewhere and push this button on the remote," Andy said, pulling out a small remote.

"That shit look weak."

"We gonna find out today," Andy said, seeing a beautiful Mexican woman get out of the Audi with a phat ass, long hair, sunglasses, and a Birkin bag on her arm.

"This freak bitch about to go in a sex store, bro. Damn, you see that ass on her?" Smurf said.

"Nigga, focus, and hold me down. If you see her, then beep the horn," Andy said, getting out walking to the Audi.

The Audi driver door window was down, so he opened the door and slid the device under the car's seat.

"Easy," Andy said, climbing back into the Mustang.

"You think you always got shit figured out to the tea," Smurf said, sounding like a hater.

"Someone is jealous!"

"Whatever. Look, here she goes," Smurf said looking at how thick she was; her pussy busting out her jeans.

"We're gonna wait, keep following her," Andy said.

Smurf followed the Audi all the way to an elementary school. The woman was Alvarado's wife and mother of his two kids, a boy and girl.

"Oh, this is going to be a movie. Bro, on the gang. You is a sick muthafucker. You trying kill kids and all," Smurf said, seeing Andy had no type of remorse.

"You have to kill bloodlines, kids and all, so nobody will come back years later to hunt you down because kids don't forget about shit. Word to life, son," Andy said agreeing with himself. He watched as Alvarado's wife put her kids in the truck. The Audi truck pulled off halfway down the busy traffic street because families were coming to pick up their kids.

BOOM!!!

The Audi blew up into a big explosion, catching on fire and the impact killed five others. Everybody was yelling, screaming, and trying to see if they saved the driver and kids in the Audi. However, their body parts were all dismembered.

***

Killers on Elm Street

Manhattan, NY

Priest Padilla Garcia ran a Roman Catholic church. He was from Puerto Rico, but he lived in New York for forty-eight years of his seventy-six years on earth. He was a very religious man with dark secrets. It was time for him to go home to his wife and closed the church until early morning hours.

The church was empty but when he heard a knock at his office door, he closed his laptop which was child porn.

"Hello," Priest Padilla Garcia said, opening the door to see a young man with a gun pointing at him

"Sit down, Priest please," Wolf said in a cold demeanor.

"Oh, Lord. Young man, I am a servant of the Lord. You are making a big mistake," the Priest said sitting down, shaken.

"Save the religious shit for someone who cares. Now, do you know why I'm here?"

"No, I don't deal with criminals or killers," Priest said, looking at Wolf open his laptop. "No, don't do that!" the priest shouted.

"You sick fuck! Wow!" Wolf said, seeing two grown men gangbang a young girl no older than twelve years old crying while pinned down to a bed.

"That must be a computer virus or pop up. I don't know how that got there," he said, lying.

"Tell me why Aguilera wants you dead?" Wolf asked, sitting on the edge of his desk to see photos of young kids mainly boys everywhere.

"Aguilera?" he replied with lust in his eyes.

"I assume you know him."

"He was my first, and the best I ever had. I still have dreams about how tight and gifted he was," the Priest said.

"I'm not fully understanding. Your first?"

"Well you see, I sometimes help young men find their inner sexual truth. Some call it gay or a creep for what I do, but I'm just giving back," the Priest said, making Wolf sick to his stomach.

"This is some *XXX Broke Back Mountain* shit!" Wolf said, not trying to hear no more. Wolf fired three bullets into his face. On his way out, he stopped and emptied the whole clip into his face.

"Nasty fuck," Wolf said to himself, walking out closing the door behind him taking off his gloves.

Chapter 32

Beacon, NY

"Gurl, this nigga. The man in Yonkers got a big bag," Lenathe said, scrolling through Andy's IG page and seeing him flashing stacks of money, rocking big chains, and a bust down Rolex.

"Damn, he's not that cute but his money makes him look like eye candy, bitch," Lenathe's friend, Porsha, said as she looked at Andy's pictures with her.

"Yeah, but he got a good personality. I can't wait to go on this early date in the morning."

"What, you really be going on dates?"

"No, tomorrow is our first one. He planned a little boat trip on the Hudson River."

"Bitch, you can't swim."

"I know, but I'ma let him swim in this pussy," Lenathe said, dapping hand with her friend.

Lenathe was a beautiful redbone, petite short, long goldish hair, dimples, nice B cup breast, and chinky eyes. She was from Mount Vernon but lived in Yonkers with her boyfriend when she wasn't at her best friend, Porsha's, house in Beacon.

"Gurl, your boyfriend is going to kill you. I'm telling you, Lenathe. You know how crazy he gets over you."

"Fuck him! All them bitches he be having, plus Andy going be my meal ticket as soon as I put this wetness on him," she said with confidence.

"Okay, but let's go out tonight. My girl said there is a big party in Newburg for a nigga named Spice who came home, and I use to fuck with him back in the day," Porsha said smiling thinking of her old boo.

"He could be the father to one of the four kids you got," Lenathe said getting up from the couch

"Bitch, please. All their fathers are accounted for. That's why I get four child support checks a month."

"You is a real hood rat."

"Yep!" Porsha replied, inhaling a blunt of weed while the kids were in their rooms sleep.

***

Yonkers, NY

Andy pulled his Benz up to the parking lot of a boat dock where he rented a pontoon boat for the morning so he could spend some time with Lenathe.

There was no denying the fact that she was the bomb. When he saw her at the beach a couple of weeks ago, he had to have her. She was a head-turner.

With so much going on, Andy forgot he had to live life and enjoy his wealth. But he planned to go out and celebrate Smurf's birthday tonight with Wolf.

Andy wanted to introduce the two men to each other because that was his circle. He'd been chilling with Wolf a lot lately and he took a strong liking to him.

"Babe!" Lenathe yelled, climbing out of an Uber, and hugging him.

"What's up, sexy?" he said looking at her sexy little frame in her booty shorts and a tank top.

"You got twenty dollars, so I can pay for the Uber?" she asked with no shame in her game. Andy passed her a wad of money totaling over $2,000.

"That's for you."

"Thanks, daddy," she said stuffing the money in her loose bra.

They climbed on the pontoon boat and took off on the beautiful sunny morning down the Hudson River leading into New Jersey.

"This is so sweet, Andy. I can't lie. I want you to fuck the shit out of me, but I just caught my period. Unless you want to run this red light?" she asked, sitting in a chair watching him steer the boat hoping he says yes.

"It's cool, ma. I just want to spend some time with you," Andy said looking back at the lust in her eyes.

"Can I at least suck your dick? My head game is crazy, and I swallow everything," she said, licking her lips.

"I'ma find out soon enough. But tell me more about who you are, love," he asked.

"Well, as you know, I live with a nigga. I work at Wendy's, no kids, and I want a better life."

"I feel you, love. Everything will fall in place. Just be patient, ma. I got you."

"I got you too," she said standing up to kiss him.

"You swim?"

"Hell, nah. Nigga, I hate water," she replied.

"You see that jellyfish?" Andy said pointing in the river.

"No, where?" Lenathe said looking into the water with him.

"Right here, baby," Andy said, pointing closer into the ocean. When Lenathe was close enough, Andy pushed her in the water.

"Andy, help me! I can't swim," she cried trying to keep from drowning.

"Where can I find Champ, bitch? And you better not lie."

"Andy, please, I'ma drown," she cried, going under the water, and coming back up scared for her life.

"You better start talking. Where is he?"

"He lives in Jersey City, the projects on 71st Street. Please, that's all I know, Andy!" she yelled, going under the water again and drowning.

Andy hit the gas on the boat, leaving her to drown in the river and heading back to Yonkers. He knew she was Champ's girlfriend for over two years. She was his side bitch, but he kept her close.

He followed her to Jones Beach and bagged her with ease, but she didn't lead him to Champ. It was like he disappeared.

Getting her to come out here was the best idea he could come up with to squeeze information out of her.

"G's up, hoes down. Your bitch can't swim, she gon' drown," Andy sang the Jim Jones song to himself out loud.

Romell Tukes

Chapter 33

Queens, NY

Club Angel's was crazy tonight all types of ballers were in the strip club tossing money. There were people in all types of professions, everybody from rappers, NBA players, and drug dealers.

Andy knew the club promoter, so he was able to throw a small party for Smurf's 23rd birthday. Smurf knew a lot of people in the city, mostly all Blood Brim gang members from his set.

Yonkers was in the building tonight half of Elm Street was on the dance floor near the two bars tossing money at the stripper sliding up and down the poles working the crowd.

"Thanks for coming out, bro. It's nice to meet you. Andy talks good about you," Smurf said to Wolf who was sitting next to him in the VIP section while Andy was at the bar throwing bands on the stage.

"Happy Birthday! You only turn 23 once, MJ," Wolf said scanning the jammed pack club. There were so many people on the floor everybody was on somebody.

"Fact bro, but what's poppin' with CB? His name is heavy up top. That's the big hat," Smurf said drinking out the biggest bottle of Henny the club had to offer.

"He's doing well. I went to check him recently," Wolf said seeing CB was drinking himself into a coma, but it was his day.

"Question?" Smurf said with a long slur.

"Talk about it."

"I heard you graduated from college. Why are you living like us when you can do so much better with your life? You made a way for yourself. Why redirect your own destiny?" Smurf asked.

"Let's just say I made a deal with the devil because I had no choice. Once I lost my sister, my life left with her," Wolf said honestly.

"Okay, I don't understand, but me and Andy with you... Have a drink, nigga. All the liquor is free," Smurf said realizing his own bottle was empty to its last drop.

"I don't drink or do drugs."

"Oh, sober life," Smurf said, seeing a beautiful bottle girl with Spanish features approach the table with a med size bottle of Henny open and a bottle of D'usse in an ice bucket.

"Here Papi. This is on the house. Happy birthday," the sexy bottle girl said wear a tank top and booty short with tats on her thighs and ass

When she dropped the bottles off, she looked back before rushing off into the dark club.

"Free bottles? A nigga feel important. I need to call some hoes in here," Smurf said reaching for the bottle of Henny, but Wolf snatched the bucket off the table. "Damn, my nigga. I thought you didn't drink," Smurf said drunk

"Look, something ain't right. Go get Andy and tell him to take you home," Wolf said helping Smurf up calling four niggas from Yonkers over to the VIP to take Smurf outside.

When Smurf and Andy were leaving the club trying to figure out what was up with Wolf, he had his eyes on the bottle girl who was sneaking into the women's restroom.

Wolf made his way through the crowd towards the bathroom. Once at the women's bathroom door, he rushed in with his gun to see the bottle girl on the phone talking in Spanish and getting dressed in an all-black outfit.

She hung up the phone with a nervous look.

"You can't be in here," she said.

"Who sent you?" Wolf said, aiming his gun at her.

"Does it matter? You're going to kill me anyway."

"Maybe not," he said looking into her sexy face.

"He paid me $100,000 to poison your friend's drink, but not yours. I don't even believe he knows who you are," she stated.

"Who?"

"Alvarado."

"You was going to leave out that window, huh? Just like that," Wolf said staring at the open bathroom window.

"That was the plan, handsome."

"Not tonight…"

Bloc! Bloc! Bloc! Bloc!
Wolf filled her chest up with ammo. Her body flew into the wall sliding down in slow motion with tears rolling down her face before everything went black. Wolf grabbed her cell phone and climbed out the bathroom window. He ran to the front of the club to see six cars parked waiting for him as if something was about to pop off everybody had guns out.

"Yo what the fuck, son? What's going on?" Wolf said, thinking there was some smoke in the club.

"They tried to poison Smurf, but we have to go. I took care of it," Wolf said while civilians came running out of the club in chaos.

Andy and Wolf climbed in the GMC truck with Smurf knocked out snoring in the back.

***

White Plains Mall
Days Later

"About time you take a bitch shopping again," Erica said, walking on the two-level of the mall filled with designer stores.

"Sorry, love. I've been so busy you have no clue, but you know my intentions are good for us. Baby, I just want you to have a perfect life," Andy said.

"Yeah and I'm thankful. But what is good of all of this if you go to jail or worse?" she said. That was the main concern she thought about all day.

"I know what you're saying, baby, but I don't plan to live like this forever."

"Nigga, that's what they all say. Shit, that's what my brother said before he was murdered. Like y'all niggas be so selfish," she said.

"Baby chill out. You have nothing to worry about because I'm not going nowhere. Let's go up in this Dolce and Gabbana store," he said.

"You can't cover up the truth with designer clothes or jewelry," she said.

"So, you want to leave?"

"Hell, nah. Nigga, you going spend some bands on my all my pain and suffering," she said laughing.

"I bet," he said walking into the clothing store.

Erica grabbed a couple of outfits to try on while Andy brought some shoes, jeans, and shorts for the summer.

"Baby, come in here," Erica said inside the dressing room.

Andy went into her dressing room booth to see her in a sexy, tight, red mini dress showing her curves and nicely shaped ass.

"How do I look, baby?" she said, seeing his hard-on. "Oh, I guess you like it," she said walking up to him rubbing his dick. She pulled his dick out, got on her knees, swirling her tongue around his dick, and then gulping him back in forth down her throat.

Not wanting to spoil the surprise, she pulled him out her mouth when she felt him about to cum.

Erica lifted her skirt and he slid into her wet walls which felt like heaven.

"Ummm yesss," she moaned, spreading her ass cheeks letting him go deeper. Andy pounded her pussy out thrusting his dick deep in her gushy love box.

"Excuse me. Only one person is allowed in the dressing room at a time," an employee said from outside the door.

Once they both came, they quickly got dressed and opened the door to see seven people staring at them. Erica couldn't help but blush while fixing her hair.

Chapter 34

Brewster, NY

"This seems a little risky, baby," Katrina told Black who was watching the bank in upstate New York.

"It's going to work. Just make sure you wear your wig and contacts, the hazel/orange ones," Black said in his zone ready to hit a TD Bank, which was the easiest type of bank in America.

"Baby, how do you rob so many banks and not get locked up?"

"Timing," he said, getting out the Ford pickup truck, dressed in a business suit, and looking very professional with a clean cut. Black only saw four civilians, two bank tellers, and one guard sitting down near the exit on his phone bored.

"Good morning, sir. Welcome to TD Bank. I'm Celine. How may I help you?" an older Spanish woman said smiling.

"I have a deposit slip," he said, passing her a note.

She read the note that said:

"Bitch give me all the money in the private safe and don't push no buttons or I'll kill you, bitch! :)" Her face frowned after reading the letter. Black flashed her his gun on his waistline under his blazer for good measures.

"I'll be right with you. I'll get everything together, sir, but I have three kids at home," she said letting him know she was trying to live.

Black looked at the other bank teller who was talking to someone about overdue transactions and deadline fees.

"Here you go, sir. Here is your $123,500," she said handing him the money in stacks.

"You dumb bitch you should have put it in a bag."

"All the bags had dye bombs in it," she claimed.

Black stuffed the money in all his pockets in a rush. The other bank teller looked at him and so was the guard who stood up to see something was odd about the man in the suit.

Black turned around to see the guard coming his way. He grabbed Katrina, who was a couple of feet next to him.

"Excuse me, sir," the security guard shouted. When he saw Black put Katrina in a chokehold with a gun to her head, he went for his work gun.

"Back the fuck up or I'll kill this bitch!" Black screamed with a crazy look in his eyes while Katrina started to cry.

"Sir, let the woman go, please. We can talk about it," the guard said while following Black who was back paddling out the exit door.

"Stop following me," Black said. Seeing the guard wasn't backing down, so he fired a shot, shooting the guard into his shoulder. Black made his exit with Katrina in tow, dragging her outside into the pickup truck.

Once Katrina was in the truck, the guard came outside shooting hitting Black in his back.

Black shot six rounds back, hitting the security guard in his head. Black hoped in the truck races off jumping on the highway under the bridge at the nick of time because cop cars were speeding across the bridge sixty deep.

"Baby, you're shot," Katrina said, seeing a big bloody hole in his upper back.

"I know we have to switch seats when I get to Jefferson County the next exit. We have to go to your mom since she's a nurse," Black said in pain.

"Yeah, but you know she going to ask all types of questions," Katrina said knowing her mom was nosey.

"And you know she doesn't like you!"

"We're going to tell her that I got hit by a stray bullet," Black stated.

***

Lower Eastside, NY

Aguilera was under the Manhattan bridge waiting for Wolf to arrive and he was already twenty minutes late.

Since meeting Wolf, life has been amazing for him and work was good. However, his partner, Agent Scott, had been speaking to Internal Affairs and he didn't know about what. Agent Scott told Aguilera they questioned him about the killing of a powerful kingpin in Staten Island.

Aguilera wondered why he wasn't questioned, but he planned to do more investigating when he had time.

He saw HD lights pull up from a black Maserati with tints and rims. Wolf climbed out making his way to Aguilera thinking about what the priest said about Aguilera.

"You're late."

"I'm never late because I don't believe in time. So, what you got for me?"

"You've been doing a good job, but none of these assholes told you anything. Did they? Because they're all liars," Aguilera asked with an awkward facial expression as if he was going to kill Wolf if he said yes.

"No, not at all. But when I do, I'll be sure to report to you."

"Thank you."

"How your ass feel? I mean calf," Wolf said correcting himself with a smirk, but Aguilera had an ace bandage around his calf from pulling a muscle in his leg

"Better. I was jogging and I pulled it, but I heal quick."

"I bet you do," Wolf said with a sarcastic tone in his voice thinking about what the priest told him.

"Here is your next task they call him Vinny from Brooklyn he's an old Mafia boss very connected he runs a chain of pizza shops called Vinny's pizza all over the city. He uses his storefronts as a front to use drugs so he's sitting on a lot of drugs." Aguilera stated, handing Wolf a folder with everything he'll need to know to get the job done.

"Okay it will be done soon, boss man," Wolf said, walking off.

Aguilera stood there starting to grow hate for him, but he couldn't kill him. At least not yet because he needed him.

Romell Tukes

Chapter 35

Brooklyn, NY

Vinny was cleaning up his pizza shop after a long day of work. It was close to 10:30 pm so the day was typically over.

Vinny was in his late sixties and a grumpy old man; he was still an active mobster member with very long connections. He controlled most of the Brooklyn drug trade thanks to his new plug. He owned four pizza shops around New York City.

Every pizza shop he owned was his stash spot or where he did his drug transactions. Two weeks ago, the FEDs did a mob sweep, arresting twenty-one of his workers from his crime family.

The shop was closed, but Vinny was wiping down the tables. He saw a black kid standing at the door trying to get in for some pizza.

"We're closed, get the fuck outta here!" Vinny shouted in his strong Italian accent waving the kid off so he could keep it moving.

When Vinny saw he wasn't going anywhere, he went to the door.

"You deaf buddy? We're closed," Vinny said, opening the door with an attitude.

"I didn't come for pizza, go back inside," Wolf said, pulling out a pistol pointing it directly at Vinny's face, forcing him into the pizza shop turning off the lights.

"This must be a mistake you have no clue who you're about to rob, but the money is in the cash register. Take that and get the fuck out!" Vinny said sitting down.

"Vinny, Vinny, Vinny... you have it all wrong. I'm here to kill you," Wolf said sitting down across from him.

"I guess this is the part where I beg for my life or ask who sent you," Vinny said with a devilish grin.

"You must have lived a good life."

"If you only knew. I killed so many people and sent hits to so many families, I wouldn't have a clue who sent you. But I don't deal with too many blacks, so this is new."

"Aguilera sent me."

"That bitch ass spick."

"Nobody likes him."

"Kid, you have no clue what type of snake you're dealing with. He will use you and throw you away like trash," Vinny said.

"So I heard, but that's neither here nor there. I came to do a job," Wolf said, pulling his trigger five times into his face. Wolf watched Vinny's head slam on to the table, leaking blood onto the floor.

Wolf couldn't leave his body just lying there, so he dragged him to the back. The only place he saw to store his body was in the oven. Wolf placed Vinny in a large, brown, stone oven which was already set to four-hundred and fifty degrees.

Wolf looked into the back office to see two duffle bags under a desk. When he looked inside, he saw stacks of white square keys with stamps of sharks branded on the keys.

"Merry Christmas to me," Wolf said, picking up the bags, leaving no forensic evidence on the crime scene. On his way out he could smell burning skin and flesh.

***

Bronx, NY

"I think we're here, bro. Wake up," Andy told Smurf, punching his shoulder. He found parking in the Parkchester area in front of a nice two-story house at the end of the block.

"A'ight," Smurf said. He was waking up out of his deep sleep because he had a long night at Juve in Brooklyn, which was the West Indian Parade and Celebration that lasted for three days.

"This gotta be smooth, but something tells me he's going to have some shit in here. Play it cool because they're going to pat us down, so we leave the grips in the car," Andy said.

"Nigga, you wilding. Son, I'm not leaving my burner in the whip." Smurf shot back looking at Andy like he lost his mind.

"Bro, you have to or they're going to think we're on some bullshit. We're just going in there to find out if he's holding, bro."

"Then after that, we come back and put in some work," Smurf said, finishing his sentence.

"Facts. Shantell said her girl had been fucking this nigga for five years and he got the Bronx on lock."

"A'ight, I'm with you," Smurf said, getting out of the car.

Three Spanish niggas opened the door and patted Andy and Smurf without saying a word. After the pat-down, they brought them to the kitchen where a Spanish man was sitting at a counter watching his flat screen tv hanging from his wall.

"Welcome. Which one of you is Andy?" the middle-aged Spanish man said in a Versace outfit looking like he was fresh from the Dominican Republic.

"Me, nice to meet you," Andy said.

"Have a seat. I'm Chino, my side chick tells me that you're looking for some work?"

"Yeah, we're trying to cop some weight and take over the city," Andy said.

"Okay, where y'all from son? I like y'all vibes," Chino said while his security posted up behind him like he was a prince.

"We from Y.O.," Smurf said.

"Yonkers? Okay, my homie Chop is from out there. My Latin King brother," Chino stated.

"I heard of him," Andy said.

"Yeah, he's in the FEDs now, but y'all must not be from Elm Street. Shit's crazy over there," Chino said.

"Nah, we from across town. But let's talk business. How much are you going to sell us a key for?" Andy asked.

"Slow down, Pop. I'm just trying to build a friendship," Chino said.

"Friends and business don't mix," Andy said.

"I agree but before we come to any business terms, I have one small question," Chino said.

"What's up? We got cash money," Smurf said.

"Why y'all do that to Flaco? It's a lot of money on y'all head. Flaco's sister is my plug, so this is a gift and a curse," Chino said, pulling out a 9mm and his guards pulling out their weapons.

Andy and Smurf were at a loss for words. They got caught lacking in their own game plan.

"This is how it is," Smurf said.

"Flaco was my people, you see how small the city is," Chino said looking back and forth at both men.

When Chino's side bitch told him about two Yonkers niggas looking for weight, he knew they had to be the dudes Flaco's sister was looking for because of her brother's murder.

Andy saw a shadow moving outside of Chino's backyard. He tried to keep his eyes on Chino until shots went off, shattering his glass slide doors.

BOOM! BOOM! BOOM! BOOM! BOOM! BOOM! BOOM! BOOM!

The gunman killed the guards, leaving Chino for last, walking into the kitchen. Chino was about to lift his gun until Smurf punched him in his face, kicking Chino and his gun on the floor.

Wolf kicked Chino's gun out the way and stood over him with a 12-gauge double-barrel shotgun.

"Check the crib for the work," Wolf said.

"Everything is under the mattress upstairs. Let me live, bro please. I'll go back to the DR, please," Chino cried with tears.

BOOM!

Chino's tears were silenced with the shotgun bullets ripping into his chest.

It took Smurf and Andy less than five minutes to clean out his stash and hop back on the highway to Yonkers. Wolf was tailing Andy because he wanted to see if he would lead him to Champ, but instead, he brought him into another murder scene.

Chapter 36

Southside, Yonkers

Club Sosa was one of the hottest Latina clubs in Yonkers and Shantell was having a good time drinking and chilling with her girls. She barely spent time in Yonkers with her three friends since she moved to the Bronx, but tonight, she was glad she came out.

Things with Smurf was good besides catching him cheating a couple of times, but she knew how niggas was. They were just like dogs roaming around until they found their way home.

"Oh my God! Girl, I'm drunk as fuck. I can't drive," Jenn said leaning on the bar trying to dance to the new "Bad Bunny" song.

"I'll drive you home. Let me go get Yassy and Maya," Shantell said seeing her other two girls walking over to them.

"Y'all hoes ready? Jenn, look at you," Yassy said, looking at her sister vomit under the bar.

"It's time to go. I'm twisted, Mami," Maya said, leaning on Shantell who only had a couple of shots of dark liquor.

"I gotta take all you bitches home," Shantell said.

"Not me. I'm leaving with that Dominican nigga by the DJ booth, so I'll see you later," Maya said the best looking one out of the bunch. She was Brazilian with a badass body, long hair that was pulled back in a ponytail with green eyes, brown skin, and big DD breast.

When she saw Maya walk out of the club, she helped Yassy and Jenn who were both outside drunk. They were blowing her high, but she knew this was part of going out with her girls.

Outside, Jenn fell down five stairs laughing, but she hurt her ankle. Shantell and Yassy helped her up then stepped off the curb to see a jeep pull up in front of them with Mexicans inside.

Boc! Boc!

"Ahhhhhahhh"

Boc! Boc! Boc! Boc! Boc! Boc! Boc! Boc! Boc! Boc!

The Jeep screeched its tires racing off while people came outside to see what was going on.

Shantell was the only one moving.

"She is alive! Get help!" Maya yelled, running to Shantell's aid, stepping over Yassy and Jenn's dead bodies. She began trying to save her best friend by flipping her on her back and putting pressure on her wounds.

"I don't want to die," Shantell whispered hear sirens.

"I won't let you! Hold on," Maya said, crying.

***

Las Piedras, Puerto-Rico
Weeks Later

"This is so beautiful. How did you even find this place, baby?" Bella asked, looking out the balcony onto the beach with island crystal clear water.

"I've been planning this trip for weeks. It's your birthday weekend, so why not!" Wolf said unpacking in the private beach house he rented for the weekend to spend time with her.

Things had been rough in life for Bella at work. She had no idea that being a cop would be this hard, but she refused to let it break her.

"I love this bed," she said, laying across the bed opening her legs a little, so he can see that she wore no panties.

"Oh yeah? That's how you feel," he said feeling his dick raise like the moon.

"I want to feel you in my mouth and pussy," she said sitting up on the bed.

Wolf wore shorts, so it was easy to undress. When he saw the look in her eyes, he knew what she wanted, and he was pleased to give it to her. Bella took his dick into her warm mouth slowly teasing him and taking him in and out her mouth. She moved her head faster and faster down his dick feeling his build-up while deep throating him and sucking at the same time and listening to his moans.

When he came, she caught his thick load swallowing every drop the way he liked.

"You beat the record," he said climbing into her open legs leaving her dress and heels on because that turned him on.

"Fuck me good. Daddy please," she begged.

Wolf stroked her sweet soaked pussy with the tip of his dick.

"Ssshhh…" she moaned while he teased her back. She raised her hips into his dick while he began to fuck her good making her pelvis bone slam into his. Wolf went deeper into her thin slit opening her walls muscle

"Ugh shit," she cried, grabbing the bed rails as he thrust deeper into her pulsing body with every motion.

He pushed her legs back and began putting an assault on her pussy

"Oh fuck! Oh, fuck yes! Romeo, I love you! Oh, shit! Baby, I'm cumming! Pleaseee fuck me!" she yelled at the top of her lungs while cumming on his dick. A waterfall of cream poured out her pussy. Wolf went down south on her and ate her so good that he was milking her cum out her tasteful pussy.

Wolf bent her over, loving the sight of her round wide-spread ass, which looked crazy when she arched her back.

"Relax baby. This may hurt a little," Wolf said raising her hips a little more in the air and spreading her soft ass cheeks.

He slapped his dick on her ass cheeks.

"Mhm, daddy! Yessss," she moaned, playing with her clit. Wolf slowly entered the tip into her tiny anus.

"Relax," he said, feeling her ass tightening on his dick. He dug deeper into her ass, feeling her loosen up as she moaned. Wolf grabbed her long hair and started to fuck her ass like a pussy.

"Ohhh baby, fuck that ass!" she yelled in her zone rolling her hips back feeling the pleasure and pain from his long strokes in her.

Bella bounced her ass on his while he came inside her ass and pulled out to see his juices pouring out her ass. When he was done, Bella put his dick back in her mouth and gave him head for an hour. After getting her face fucked, she rode his dick until it was lights out.

Romell Tukes

Chapter 37

Elm Street, Yonkers

Dirt bikes and sport bikes flew up and down the block, the best riders were out today. The Ruff Ryders were everywhere on their bikes, showing off for the death of Mark who died in a bike accident years ago.

"The block litty today, bro," Andy told T-Bay and a couple of his young boys shooting dice in front of a building.

"Facts, son. But yo', what's good with Shantell?" T-Boy asked. He'd been friends with Andy, Smurf, and Shantell since kids.

"Facts. We're ready, but I'm done with them keys. The bread is upstairs. That shit has been moving like hotcakes," T-Boy said, placing his dreads in a ponytail.

T-Boy was a twenty-five-year-old hustler who gave up his hoop dreams for the streets. He was 6'6" and skilled with the ball. He was the Rucker's MVP last year for his dunking skills.

"I'ma holler at Smurf because I ran out and niggas ain't got no plug."

"Stop robbing them then you may have one," T-Bay said already knowing how Andy got down. Shit, the whole city did.

"Facts. But if I don't go out and get it, who gonna feed us?" Andy said with his back to the street. T-Boy was about to say something until he saw a Ford Focus racing down the street with a gun pointing out the window.

"Duck," T-Boy said, shooting first and then the whole block started shooting at the car getting the driver in his neck.

The Ford crashed into a car and a Mexican hoped up shooting, killing two little niggas on the block before they rained on his body. Over forty rounds sprayed into the Mexican, killing him.

Everybody ran off, clearing the block before shit got flooded with police.

***

Meanwhile
Across Town

Wolf just got back from Puerto Rico with Bella and he had the time of his life. He never knew how beautiful Puerto Rico was until now. He wanted to go back in a couple of months just to get away. Bella questioned him about all the money he had lately, and the new Maserati was all he was hearing about.

Wolf told her his brother was holding him down and she believed him. Money had been coming so fast. He made six bank accounts in foreign countries like he read in a *Hide Your Money* self-help book.

He climbed in his Maserati to see a letter in his seat. He looked around the garage to see if anybody was around because someone had to break into his car to place the letter inside. He always locked his car door because Yonkers niggas were car thieves. It read...

"Dear Wolf,

How was your trip to Puerto Rico? I'm sure you had fun with my daughter, but it's back to work. The name and address are at the bottom of this shit.

Be easy,

Big O from 138 Nick St."

Wolf put the piece of paper in his pocket and opened his glove compartment to put his pistol inside. When he closed it, he saw Bella standing outside of his car door, scaring the shit out of him.

"Babe, what the fuck? You scared the hell out of me," he said, rolling down his tinted windows. She could see through if she looked hard enough.

"You forgot this," she said, passing him his Louis Vuitton wallet.

"Thank you, baby."

"What were you doing?" she asked.

"What are you talking about?"

"In your glove compartment," she said dressed in her police uniform. Her walkie-talkie called in a code, asking for all available units to respond. "I have to go. Love you," she said, running off to her car because she was on break. Wolf made her a lunch upstairs that they just enjoyed.

Wolf's heart was racing like he just did a crime but if Bella was to see he had a gun she would go crazy.

***

Harlem, NY

Wolf parked on the one-way street full of brownstones, looking for #85 and it was in front of him.

Wolf walked into the brownstone and up the three flights of stairs to see apartment three's door was wide open. Wolf peaked his head inside to see a Spanish chick in a red dress from the back with the biggest ass he ever saw.

He dick started to jump watching her walk back and forth because her ass wobbled and bounced with every step. He heard her talking in Spanish on the phone to someone while placing a duffle bag on the table.

Wolf walked inside the apartment, creeping on her. "Get off the phone," Wolf said, putting the gun to her head from behind. She hung up and said nothing

"Take it," she said with base in her voice.

"Turn around," Wolf said, backing up. When she started around, Wolf almost threw up on himself looking at the transgender who had double DD breasts and thick curves. Her eyes were hazel, and she had a soft feminine look, but his Adam's apple was bigger than Wolf's.

"What, you thought I was Beyonce?" the tranny said.

"Why did Aguilera send me here?" he asked him.

"Oh, no he didn't! He's going to get his one day. I gave him my heart and love. I sucked his dick for over ten years and let him fuck me every way. That's why I got..."

Bloc! Bloc! Bloc!

Wolf blew his brain out onto the dining room table, hearing enough. He took the duffle bag and left, wondering what type of crazy shit Aguilera was on because he had some freaky shit going on.

Chapter 38

Cross County Mall
Later

Wolf was parked in the mall lot watching shoppers go in and out of the mall. He saw families and little kids, which made him think about Bella and building his own family. But there was only one problem: Aguilera.

He started to wonder if Bella was in on this blackmail investment, but he knew Bella wasn't that type of person. She was a good girl.

When he saw a Benz coupe and a Benz GG3 truck pull up across from his, he was relieved because he hated riding dirty.

Andy climbed out of the Benz looking stressed and cautious as he looked over his shoulders. He got in the passenger seat of the Maserati.

"What's good? Man, you okay?" Wolf asked.

"Hell, nah. Them fucking Mexicans just killed two of my men earlier. Now my block is hot as fish grease."

"Damn bro."

"Yeah, but I'ma handle them. I just need shit to die down because the FEDs are in town right now. I'm moving slow, but Smurf and I got shit lit in some outta town spots," Andy stated.

"Okay, well I got some shit in the back for you," Wolf said.

"Right on time, son word. I'm down to grams," Andy said.

"I got lucky. But if you need more just holler."

"Wolf, you've done enough. This is my fight, bro, but thanks."

"A'ight, I'ma go pick up some shit from the sex store."

"Freak nigga."

"Nah for wifey."

"Who you fuck with? I always see you alone."

"I know Andy and I plan to keep it like that," Wolf said ducking the question because if he was to tell a street nigga his wifey is a cop, they will look at him funny.

"Flash your lights so my goons can get the work," Andy said. Once he flashed his headlights, two hoodlums hopped out and Wolf popped his trunk for them. They got the duffle bag and climbed back into the Benz truck like nothing ever happened.

"I'll have your cut in the morning. By the way, nice car. Better than that cheap-ass Benz," Andy said, laughing and getting out of the car.

Wolf waited for him to pull off then he walked through the mall, picking up a couple of things for Bella because he knew she would be busy at work. She couldn't do her favorite thing, which was to shop.

***

An Hour Later

Wolf left the mall and it was pitch black out but still early and muggy. He planned to go home and cook dinner for Bella. He loved to cater to his girl. It was something that his mom taught him.

Before he made it to his car, he saw someone run behind a van, and then shots rang out. Wolf dropped his bags and shot back. The high-power weapon the gunman was shooting almost took his head off. Wolf ducked and hid behind a pole.

Wolf saw the gunman wore a mask and had good accuracy. The two went bullet for bullet, but nothing happened. The gunman took off into the night. Wolf hopped in his Maserati after picking up the bags for Bella that he dropped.

On his way home, all he could think about was what just took place. Everything was happening so fast, he felt like his life was slowly leaving earth. Last year, he never imagined he would become a hitman to save himself from going to prison for life.

***

Boston, MA

Black was able to land a job as a janitor in a local bank in North Boston. Since he had a clean record and a long made-up resume, he was able to get a cleaning job.

Tonight was his fourth day on the job and he was ready to handle his business. Black just got done cleaning the bathrooms downstairs. He pushed a cart full of cleaning supplies and reading material. The bank closed two hours ago and the manager who was a mid-age racist white man with a smart-ass mouth was working overtime.

"Excuse me, Mr. Burton. Would you like me to empty your garbage?" Black asked, stepping into his office.

"That's your job, isn't it?" Burten replied.

"Yes sir," Black said, grabbing the small full garbage bin.

"Where you from?"

"New York."

"Oh, a Yankee? No wonder why," Burten stated, going over some paperwork.

"I don't understand," Black said.

"Your people never understand and that's the problem. This is a white man's society. Do you understand that?" Burton said strongly with an evil look.

"Yes sir," Black said, stepping out of his office to empty his trash.

"Nigger," Burten mumbled under his breath going back to work.

Seconds later Black walked back into the room with the empty trashcan.

"About time. What you got lost in the cotton field?" Burton said, laughing.

"Yep," Black said, pulling out his gun. Burton's face went from laughs to fear in seconds. "Get the fuck up, cracker, and open the vault. You need to place everything into this," Black said, tossing him a big military-green duffle bag. Burten was so scared he did as he was told at a rapid speed.

It took seven minutes for him to fill the bag with crispy new blue faces. This was the biggest lick Black ever hit.

"Done, I'm sorry about what I said earlier," Burton said.

"Shut up, bitch, and walk out the front door," Black said, tossing the heavy bag over his shoulder with one gun trained on Burten.

When Burten opened the front door, he sprayed twelve rounds into Burton's chest then ran off down the block where Katrina was parked waiting.

Chapter 39

Jersey City, NJ

"I'ma run to the store, Champ. You need something?" Champ's cousin, Amp, asked him.

"Nah, nigga. I'm good. Just grab some boxes of dutches for this loud," Champ said, walking into the small living room in his boxers shirtless.

"A'ight and wake up Lay Lay. Tell her rachet ass that she gotta go. I don't trust that bitch. She got my little man, Mel G, knocked off," Amp said.

"That bitch's pussy is fire. Word is bond, son," Champ said, not giving a fuck what his cousin was talking about.

"A'ight," Amp said, walking out laughing because he knew Lay Lay burned half the projects.

Champ was hiding out in Jersey City in the projects they called the Bricks. It was known for its violence, drugs, and gang activity.

He had to get out of Yonkers for a while because too much shit was going on. He knew if he stayed, he would either be in jail or dead. He needed time to form a golden plan and strike.

Weeks ago, he got a call from Lenathe's friend, Reese, he was fucking on the side. She told him that Lenathe was found dead in a river and the cause of death was drowning. She also told him how Porsha told her that Lenathe was on a date with some nigga she met named Andy. When Champ heard this, he was glad days before her murder he was long gone.

Reese's main reason for calling was to get some money and dick, but Champ told her he would have to do a rain check.

Champ sat on the couch drinking a beer thinking about Andy and all the pain he caused him. Everything was well in his life until he killed that young basketball chick last year. He started to wonder if Andy had any ties to her because he felt as if he was missing something.

***

Axminster St, Yonkers

Dime had ten open keys on the table with six of his goons bagging up crack cocaine. They were cooking on the stove. Dime worked for Andy and the hood was full of crackheads; he made $25,000 a day on Axminster Street alone.

"Yo, Dime. What's up with them MGM niggas down the block? I heard they got at Snoop the other night," Young Billy said while bagging up dimes in sandwich bags.

"It's lit with them niggas, bro. I'ma send Man-Man and Rolex down there tonight. Watch the movie they put on, son," Dime said rolling up a blunt.

"Facts. That nigga Rolex be dropping shit. I saw that nigga kill two niggas in front of the courthouse last winter and he still ain't get caught," True said, standing over the stove and stirring the coke in the boiling water while adding baking soda.

"He on the run now from the shit, son. Facts," Dime said in the living room looking at all the coke and crack everywhere in his trap.

BOOM!

The crib door flew open

Tat-tat-tat-tat-tat-tat-tat-tat-tat-tat-tat-tat-tat!

Boc! Boc! Boc! Boc! Boc! Boc! Boc! Boc!

Tat-tat-tat-tat-tat-tat-tat-tat-tat-tat-tat-tat-tat!

Dime and his crew were in a vicious gun battle with the eight Mexicans who busted into the apartment.

Dime ran into his bedroom, climbed out his window, went down the fire escape, and ran down the alley, ducking shots while shooting back until his gun was empty.

The apartment was left a bloody mess with seven dead bodies, none of Dime's men survived the mayhem led by Alvarado.

***

Auburn Maximum Prison

CB and OG Chuck were outside in the yard enjoying the day walking the track.

"What's on your mind young blood," OG Chuck said, sensing something was wrong with him.

"I got so much shit on my head. I don't know where to start, son," CB said nodding his head at a couple of Gorilla Stone Bloods talking in a circle near a phone plotting something.

"Spill it nigga. I'm the prison's *Dr. Phil*. If I don't have the answers, then you asked the wrong question," OG said.

"Since my little sister died, I can feel the toll it's taking on my mom and brother. That shit hurts when a nigga loses a loved one and he can't do shit because he's caged behind a wall," CB stated.

"Sometimes we have to try to discipline our brains and exit things out of our thoughts in this type of situation because it will destroy us emotionally and mentally. You need to be 100% in here, to stay focused and block out thoughts in which you have no control over. Trust me, I've been there," OG said.

"You make sense, I can't even lie. I'ma take your advice. My other worry is this clown ass nigga, Major. He keeps spinning a nigga and that's the homie, so I give him slack and time, but he's taking me for granted. If I let him play with my money, everybody is going to think I'm sweet and then I'ma have to show them," CB said, looking at Major talking on the phone laughing and enjoying himself in a pair of new Timbs and a sweatsuit.

"CB, everybody aren't honorable niggas. We stand on morals while most of these niggas stand on nothing. Two things a nigga should never play with and that's his family and money," OG said.

"I agree. You're going back on the first go back?" CB asked, walking towards the line of phones in the yard. The yard lights came on because it was getting dark outside.

"Yeah. What's up?"

"I need you to take something back to the block for me and flush it," CB asked.

"A'ight where it's at?" OG said. He watched CB walk up to Major, spit a razor out his mouth and slash Major across his face from his ear to his lip.

"Ahhhhhhhh!" Major screamed, running off to get help. CB passed OG the bloody razor and walked off into a crowd of niggas walking the track while Major was at the C.O. booth.

Chapter 40

Putnam County, NY

Wolf pulled into the small shopping center area where Aguilera was awaiting him leaning on a GMC truck in a suit and tie looking like a real FBI Agent.

"Wolf, nice to see you," Aguilera said lying.

"I wish I could say the same, but I got a question. Who wants all these people dead, but his shit is starting to get really weird?" Wolf said, giving him a funny look.

"Life is weird, Wolf. If you must know, most of the hits that I send you on are from very, very, very powerful people, who pay a lot of money."

"You should've hired a real hitman," Wolf said, not understanding why he had to blackmail him.

"Nah that would've been too easy and too dangerous. Who would ever think you would be a killer? A college kid with a clean record?"

"Okay, I get it."

"Anywho, here is your next vic. I only have an address, but I know he's a male in the Bronx so just do how you do. Make sure it's clean and someone has been tailing you, so be cautious," Aguilera said getting inside his truck pulling off.

Wolf looked around slowly as he bent down to tie his sneaker to see a red Nissan GTR with tints that he saw too many times.

"Shit!" Wolf said because the scene with Aguilera looked fishy, but Wolf knew he was caught. Wolf took a deep breath and made his way over to the man in the parked car who was watching his every move.

Wolf knocked on the window and the driver rolled down the window.

"Get inside," Andy said, rolling back up the window while Wolf walked around the car.

"I know what it looks like but it's not like that."

"So, what is it like? Because it looks like you working for them people," Andy said, upset.

"You remember Fred's murder and Champ's family that got killed?" Wolf asked.

"Yeah."

"I did it and that Federal Agent was watching me. He caught me, but he's my girlfriend's father. He's been blackmailing me into killing powerful people or he is going to send me to jail, so I have no choice," Wolf said.

"Damn, so that's how you getting all this coke?" Andy said adding everything up.

"Yeah."

"He must be dirty."

"You have no clue," Wolf stated.

"A'ight, I thought you were a rat or something. I was going to have to kill you," Andy said seriously.

"Good, I wouldn't have it no other way," Wolf said, climbing out of the car.

***

Valhalla County Jail

Smurf was in the county jail's bullpen, pacing back and forth, pissed off and ready to scream.

His P.O. 's supervisor had just violated him for not showing up to two parole visits, but he told them he was sick with a food virus, but they weren't feeling his story.

The last thing he needed was to be in jail for a parole violation. There was a war in Yonkers with the Mexicans and his trap house on Beech Street got robbed yesterday. His little cousin got killed when three Mexicans armed with guns ran in the spot.

Days before that, Dime's spot got robbed and his little niggas got killed. Dime was a wanted man. His face was all over the news for seven murders.

Smurf picked up the payphone to call Shantell for the 20th time, but she must have been sleeping still. It was eight o'clock in the morning. He called Andy, who picked up on the second ring.

"Yo bro, I caught a violation."

"Damn, how the fuck did you do that?" Andy asked through the phone.

"I missed two visits."

"I told you to go see that white bitch. You thought shit was sweet," Andy replied.

"I know but call Shantell and let her know."

"Got you. I'll hit your books and make sure you good, bro. I got everything under control out here, son."

"A'ight good. That's all. Stay safe and rock out with Wolf."

"Facts. Call me later, I'ma try to reach Shantell. She knows what time it is," Andy said.

"A'ight bro, love you," Smurf said.

"Love you too," Andy said, hanging up on the other end of the line.

"Can I get a call, big homie?" a fat nigga said sitting on the bench staring at Smurf.

"Nigga fuck outta here. Suck my dick! What I look like, AT&T?" Smurf said walking to the window seeing C.O. 's walk back and forth in booking bringing inmates out of bullpens to change their street clothes in for an orange jumpsuit.

***

Staten Island, NY

Aguilera was driving on the highway with his ex-partner, Agent Scott, in the passenger seat on the way to their fishing trip.

"Thanks for inviting me out. You know how much I love fishing," Agent Scott said.

"Yeah it's been a while and now they got you working on them YG kids in the Bronx, we never kick it."

"I know this case is big. It's one hundred and forty-six of them all in one project. I'm going to bring them down and then I'm going for them Blood Mackballa kids," Agent Scott said.

"I'm proud of you, man. You deserve it."

"How is work for you? I was saddened when they split us up."

"Me too, but I think O.I.G. is building a case on me. Did you hear anything about that?" Aguilera said, turning onto a small county road. He looked at Agent Scott who was sweating bullets.

"Noo not at-t-t-t all," Agent Scott said fumbling over his words. "Where are we? I don't remember this area from last time."

Aguilera parked, pulled out his Glock 17, and shot Scott twice in the head. He opened his passenger door and shoved him on the ground before pulling off. He heard Scott was helping build a case on him with Internal Affairs.

Chapter 41

Bronx, NY

Wolf had been parked on the side block off White Plains Road in the Uptown section, watching the apartment building window of 4A. He saw a sexy ass Black chick in the window at times. She would leave and come back, but that was it.

He was starting to get impatient and to make matters worse, Bella was blowing up his phone. He told her that he was out of town for the night. Today, last year, was when Victoria was murdered, so he was feeling like shit.

A pizza delivery car pulled up and double-parked near the building and Wolf came up with a quick idea. He hopped out and crossed the street almost getting hit by a speeding cab.

He followed the pizza man in the lobby. Inside, he saw him carrying a bag full of pizza.

"Take off your hat and shirt," Wolf said, aiming his gun at him.

"You can have it," the nerdy kid said, taking off everything.

"Get the fuck out and leave your car."

"Okay," the pizza man said, running out the building shirtless. Wolf put on the pizza shop shirt and hat looking like a real pizza boy. Wolf took the stairs to the fourth floor with the pizza ready to be delivered. He placed his gun under the bag out of eyesight as he knocked on apartment 4A.

"Hold on," a male voice said.

Wolf heard a male voice and he knew his target was home. He wanted to make this quick, so he could get back to Yonkers before Bella went crazy.

When the door opened, Wolf almost pissed on himself while staring at his brother, Black.

"Wolf, what the fuck are you doing here?" Black asked, looking at his little brother up and down. Nobody knew where Black lived, not even his mom or brother. So, seeing him here was shocking.

"Baby, who is that?" Katrina said coming to the door looking beautiful as ever.

"My brother," Wolf stated.

"The young one? Hey, nice to finally meet you," Katrina said hugging Wolf, but he was frozen.

"Hey, I got a new pizza job and they said 4A," Wolf said.

"It says 9A right there," Black said pointing at the tag on the pizza bag which kept the pizza warm.

"Oh shit. I thought that was a four," Wolf said laughing.

"You want to come in bro?" Black asked, seeing Wolf was nervous and acting strange.

"No, it's a busy night. Call me. I'll come back sometime next week, bro," Wolf said walking off at a fast pace. Black stood there shaking his head wondering if his little brother was on drugs because he looked like he was on coke or dust, or maybe both.

***

Tarrytown, NY

Champ's mother lived in a nice house behind a private school with her mother that she took care of.

It was a nice day outside, so Caramitta brought her mom out on the porch in her wheelchair to enjoy a nice sunny day.

"I remember sixty-five years ago, I used to be in them slave fields wishing we had this type of heat in Selma, Alabama," her mom said in her raspy voice.

"Mom, this is New York."

"You was born in Alabama, child. You forgot," her mom said.

"No, mom. I didn't forget. You remind me every day," Caramitta stated.

"You damn right. Everybody got the southern roots in their blood. We used to all dream of coming up north to get away from slavery because places like New York was freeing slaves while it was getting worst in the south."

"I went to school, mommy. I know."

"Let me tell my story, baby. Stop trying to interrupt," her mom said seeing a young man walk up to their porch.

"Excuse me. Where can I find 126 Valley Street?" a young man asked them.

"Down the block here, but I don't think you want to go down there. It's a bad place," Caramitta said.

"Thank you," Andy said, pulling out a 9mm from his lower back letting off shots in Caramitta's face and her mom's upper body, killing them both. Andy walked off and climbed in his Benz racing off.

***

Mount Vernon, NY

Wolf was getting gas at an Exxon at 7 am on his way to meet Andy. He had his back turned towards the street pumping gas.

Boc! Boc! Boc! Boc!

Wolf ducked and raised with his gun to see a gray Cadillac CTS racing off down the street running red lights. This was the second time someone tried to take his head off and he had no clue who it was. He climbed in his Maserati and pulled off, now sporting two bullet holes in his driver's door.

***

Valhalla County Jail

Smurf was in the gym playing basketball with other inmates. The gym was large with thirty inmates inside from the old jail section on the third floor.

He'd been waiting on his parole hearing in two weeks to see if he would have to do his time in the county or up north.

"Time out, sub me in. I'll be back," Smurf said, stopping the game because he had to go piss. He started walking past a gang of Mexicans that were talking in Spanish.

Smurf laughed at them and went to take a piss. When he was taking a piss, he closed his eyes because it felt so good.

Two MS-13 Mexican gang members snuck in the bathroom and started stabbing Smurf up at the stall over fifty times.

When he looked dead slumped and bleeding everywhere on the floor, they made their exit. Minutes later, Smurf's homie went to take a piss to see Smurf in a pool of blood not moving and called for help.

Chapter 42

Yonkers, NY
Days Later

Wolf was in his condo sleep he had a long night with Bella full of rough sex and passionate sex. She wore him out.

He rolled over to feel a gun pointed to his forehead, waking him up.

"Good morning," Aguilera said with a gun to his head.

"Handle your shit. What you waiting for?" Wolf asked.

"You missed your target," Aguilera said standing up.

"I wasn't going to kill my brother. You know that was my brother."

"Your brother? It couldn't have been," Aguilera said with a confused look.

"It was. I don't know what type of games you playing, but I'm not killing my blood," Wolf said with bass in his voice.

"I understand that, and you don't have to, but he must have pissed someone off. I have a new mission for you and I also have a gift for you," Aguilera stated handing him a brown folder.

"Who is this? Oh shit! The fucking Mayor of Yonkers? Man, you tripping the fuck out," Wolf said getting out of bed.

"He's next, period. But look at the next photo, you remember that gray Cadillac," Aguilera asked.

"Yeah, he tried to kill me."

"While there goes all his info."

"How did you know about this? I'm not surprised if you set it up. You would have been dead, but it looks like you got more problems than you can handle," Aguilera said walking towards the door.

"Aguilera next time you put a gun to my head, you better pray you use it."

"Oh, I will. Trust me," he said leaving Wolf alone staring at the photo of the man who tried to take his life twice.

Romell Tukes

***

Southside, Yonkers

Alvarado was in a bar drinking and enjoying his night alone. He had four guards outside waiting for him. The bar only had sixteen people listening to Mexican music and playing pool. Alvarado's life was a mess. He regretted taking the position Jimenez offered him because he was doing good in Long Island, New York. Now, he lost his family and his emotions. He felt like his life was going downhill since coming to Yonkers.

He checked his Rolex watch and was ready to leave. He was a little drunk, but not to the point where he couldn't walk.

Alvarado walked out of the bar to the small parking lot across the street where his men awaited him. When he got to the van, he saw his soldiers all had bullets in his head. He reached for his gun but was too slow.

"Put your hands up and don't fucking move the wrong way or I'll blow your fucking head off," Andy said breathing down the back of his neck.

"You finally got me."

"Yep, turn your bitch ass around. You got my men stabbed up," Andy said with fire in his eyes.

"It's the art of war. You think it's the end, but it's only the beginning. You have no clue what's going on," Alvarado said.

"I love the unknown," Andy said before emptying the rest of the clip into the back of his head.

***

Cortlandt Manor, NY

Mayor Thomas lived in a rich community thirty minutes away from Yonkers where he was the city Mayor. He was forty-three years old, African American, married to a beautiful wife with two young boys ages eight and eleven years old.

Thomas was enjoying dinner with his wife and kids talking about his long day in the office.

"Baby, this food is wonderful," Thomas said, lying to his wife, but she was such a bad cook. The dogs were scared to eat her slop.

"Thank you. I spent hours in the kitchen preparing it," she replied taking big bites trying to ignore the disgusting taste herself.

"How was school today, Larry?" Thomas asked his son. When he saw the man walk into his dining room with a gun, his heart stopped.

Wolf pulled out a dining room table chair and sat down slowly.

"Mayor Thomas," Wolf said, looking at the family all staring at him with fear.

"Finish eating now," Thomas yelled to his kids who both started to eat slowly.

"Aguilera," Wolf said.

"I understand. You don't have to explain," Thomas stated, looking at his wife cry.

Boc! Boc! Boc! Boc! Boc! Boc! Boc! Boc! Boc! Boc!

Wolf killed the two boys and his wife, who flipped out her chair onto her back.

Thomas held in his tears at the sight of losing his family in such a gruesome manner.

"I hope you believe in Karma. Murdering innocent people wasn't how I taught Aguilera."

"What you mean?" Wolf asked with his gun aimed at him.

"I taught Aguilera everything he knows. I'm the only person who can mind control him. I knew you were coming before you did, kid. I don't think you truly know what you signed up for because it's deeper than what you can see," Thomas said.

"I will soon find out," Wolf said, shooting him twice in the head and getting blood all over the white walls.

Romell Tukes

Chapter 43

Goshen St, Yonkers

Mickey walked into his apartment building with a backpack after a long day of work to only come up short. He spent his whole day looking for Wolf, but he couldn't find him he checked his condo area, Elm St and around town

Mickey was a killer who got paid for his amazing work. He left a gang of bodies over his twenty-three-year profession. He was forty-one years old and he loved his work with a passion.

He was born and raised in Maryland, Prince George County, but his life and work were in New York. He was paid a large amount of money to take out Wolf and the deadline was in days. The two times he almost hit him he failed which wasn't like him because Mickey always hit his targets.

Inside his two-bedroom apartment, it was empty. He normally spent most of his time in Brooklyn, but he had a lot of work in Yonkers. Mickey grabbed a beer from his lower cabinets in his kitchen. When he plopped his head back up, he was met by Wolf's pistol.

"Who are you?" Wolf asked.

"You got the drop on me, you should know," Mickey said, opening his Budweiser beer and drinking it.

"I do, but I don't. Who sent you to kill me, Aguilera?" Wolf asked as Mickey busted out laughing.

"Aguilera? I would never do business with that faggot ass nigga. A word of advice, you shouldn't either anymore," Mickey stared into Wolf's confused eyes.

"So, who sent you?"

"I don't kiss and tell, so you're just going to have to kill me. But I will tell you this. It doesn't matter if you kill me or not."

"Why you say that? A dead man is a dead man."

"Yeah, but she won't stop at nothing to kill if she wants you dead," Mickey said, confusing him.

Mickey saw a perfect chance to rush him. He tried to fight Wolf for his weapon, but Wolf was taller and stronger, so he overpowered him. Wolf kicked Mickey onto the floor and shot him three times in his face. Wolf ran out of the apartment leaving him leaking on the floor dead.

***

Bella and her new partner were parked in an undercover car watching a notorious drug trafficking building on Goshen Street. They sat watching the fiends run in and out all day. Bella and her new partner, Harry, just heard shots go off from a building across the street. Harry and Bella jumped out of the car when they saw a man running out of the building with a gun.

"Shots fired on Goshen Street. Backup is needed!" Harry yelled into his radio closing in on the gunman.

"Freeze!" Harry said to the gunman who turned around slowly and shot Harry in his head, dropping him

"Put the gun down!" Bella yelled closing in on him about to shoot the gunman until they locked eyes. When Bella saw it was Wolf, her heart stopped.

Wolf saw her face contorted in pain, but he took off running as sirens were going off in the distance. When the police came, Harry was dead, and she told the police the shooter ran. She couldn't see his face or even get a good enough shot.

She was so shocked at what she saw, she almost passed out. She went to the hospital to find out what was wrong with her and the doctors informed her that she was pregnant.

***

An Hour Later
Levenson Street, Yonkers

Champ was in the elevator in his paternal aunt's house. He was back in Yonkers to bury his mother and grandma in a couple of days. He had just spoken to his brother, Lingo Loc, earlier who is upstate in Attica prison doing a bid. He was sick when he found out about his family.

There was no doubt in his mind who was responsible for the death of his family. He knew Andy was trying to make his life hell, but he swore to get him and everything he ever loved.

He got off the elevator and walked to his aunt's apartment. She always left the door open, so he walked right in. He made a mental note to tell her to start locking up the place.

"Auntie, I'm here," Champ said walking through the clean apartment with plastic covers over the furniture and antique vases posted in the corners.

Champ walked to the back to see her bedroom door wide open. He found her lying dead in her bed, sitting up against her wall with six bullets in her head. He cried so hard at the mere sight.

"It hurts when you see someone you love meet their fate. It makes you wish you never saw it." Wolf entered the room pointing a Draco at Champ who had tears rolling down his face. He was looking at Wolf in the mirror across the room.

"It's you," Champ said remembering Wolf's face from the high school parking lot the night he shot him and killed Victoria.

"Yeah, it's me. You killed my sister and I killed everything you loved. Your baby mother, kids, and your aunt. Oh, and I can't forget Fred, your partner in crime. I didn't kill your mom or grandma, but I'm glad Andy did because that's what I knew would bring you here to me."

"Smart," Champ replied.

"Somewhat, but I had a long night and I've been waiting for this day for over a year. I've been very patient and now look," Wolf said with a proud tone.

"You think you got it all figured out, don't you?" Champ asked.

"I do."

"You don't know shit. You're only a pawn and Aguilera is going to use you until you get him a checkmate," Champ said.

"What does Aguilera have to do with this?" Wolf asked now pissed.

"You're not that smart, little nigga. I work for Aguilera also. He paid me to kill your little sister. He knew if we were to kill her, you would come for us and kill one of us. Fred was the bait. If I would have known that you would have killed my family, I would have never done this shit. He planned this shit out to the t. Me and you both were only pawns, Wolf," Champ said.

"Why should I believe you?"

"Because it is the truth and look in my backpack by the door. I would never lie. Plus, I'm ready to die. I have nothing to live for. I killed everything I love," Champ said.

Wolf's mind was spinning as he reached for Champ's Gucci bookbag and saw a brown folder inside. When he opened the folder, he saw photos of Victoria and him.

"Told you. Aguilera is the devil, son, but it's too late to back out. You're in too deep," Champ said.

"I'll figure it out," Wolf said.

"Tell Erica that I'm sorry."

"Will do," Wolf said before shooting Champ forty-six times while thinking about Victoria. Wolf left with a new mission on his mind. He took Champ's bookbag and exited the apartment.

***

"That's him, boss," a Mexican said in the driver's seat watching Wolf come out the building. Jimenez was on the phone with someone very important from California that had a higher rank than him.

Jimenez had goons on the rooftop, in six different cars on the street, goons in apartment buildings, all ready to attack and kill Wolf at his say so.

"Are you sure?" Jimenez asked the caller. "Okay," Jimenez said, hanging up the phone, taking two deep breaths.

"Tell the men to stand down. Come to find out his father is a very powerful man and is connected to the top dawg, so he sent word to stand down. Wolf will get his sooner or later. Let's go," Jimenez said in the back seat of his Rolls Royce Phantom...

To Be Continued…
Killers on Elm Street 2
Coming Soon

Submission Guideline

Submit the first three chapters of your completed manuscript to ldpsubmissions@gmail.com, subject line: Your book's title. The manuscript must be in a .doc file and sent as an attachment. Document should be in Times New Roman, double spaced and in size 12 font. Also, provide your synopsis and full contact information. If sending multiple submissions, they must each be in a separate email.

Have a story but no way to send it electronically? You can still submit to LDP/Ca$h Presents. Send in the first three chapters, written or typed, of your completed manuscript to:

LDP: Submissions Dept
Po Box 944
Stockbridge, Ga 30281

DO NOT send original manuscript. Must be a duplicate.

Provide your synopsis and a cover letter containing your full contact information.

Thanks for considering LDP and Ca$h Presents.

Killers on Elm Street

BOW DOWN TO MY GANGSTA

By **Ca$h**

TORN BETWEEN TWO

By **Coffee**

THE STREETS STAINED MY SOUL **II**

By **Marcellus Allen**

BLOOD OF A BOSS **VI**

SHADOWS OF THE GAME II

TRAP BASTARD II

By **Askari**

LOYAL TO THE GAME **IV**

By **T.J. & Jelissa**

IF LOVING YOU IS WRONG… **III**

By **Jelissa**

TRUE SAVAGE **VIII**

MIDNIGHT CARTEL IV

DOPE BOY MAGIC IV

CITY OF KINGZ III

By **Chris Green**

BLAST FOR ME **III**

A SAVAGE DOPEBOY III

CUTTHROAT MAFIA III

DUFFLE BAG CARTEL VI

HEARTLESS GOON VI

By **Ghost**

A HUSTLER'S DECEIT III

KILL ZONE **II**

BAE BELONGS TO ME III

A DOPE BOY'S QUEEN III

By **Aryanna**

COKE KINGS V

KING OF THE TRAP II

By **T.J. Edwards**

GORILLAZ IN THE BAY V

3X KRAZY III

De'Kari

THE STREETS ARE CALLING II

Duquie Wilson

KINGPIN KILLAZ IV

STREET KINGS III

PAID IN BLOOD III

CARTEL KILLAZ IV

DOPE GODS III

Hood Rich

SINS OF A HUSTLA II

ASAD

KINGZ OF THE GAME VI

Playa Ray

SLAUGHTER GANG IV

RUTHLESS HEART IV

By **Willie Slaughter**

FUK SHYT II

By **Blakk Diamond**

TRAP QUEEN

By **Troublesome**

YAYO V

GHOST MOB II

Stilloan Robinson

KINGPIN DREAMS III

By Paper Boi Rari

CREAM II

By Yolanda Moore

SON OF A DOPE FIEND III

By Renta

FOREVER GANGSTA II

GLOCKS ON SATIN SHEETS III

By Adrian Dulan

LOYALTY AIN'T PROMISED III

By Keith Williams

THE PRICE YOU PAY FOR LOVE III

By Destiny Skai

I'M NOTHING WITHOUT HIS LOVE II

SINS OF A THUG II

By Monet Dragun

LIFE OF A SAVAGE IV

MURDA SEASON IV

GANGLAND CARTEL IV

CHI'RAQ GANGSTAS IV

KILLERS ON ELM STREET II

By **Romell Tukes**

QUIET MONEY IV

EXTENDED CLIP III

By **Trai'Quan**

THE STREETS MADE ME III

By **Larry D. Wright**

IF YOU CROSS ME ONCE II

ANGEL III

By **Anthony Fields**

Romell Tukes

FRIEND OR FOE III

By **Mimi**

SAVAGE STORMS III

By **Meesha**

BLOOD ON THE MONEY III

By **J-Blunt**

THE STREETS WILL NEVER CLOSE II

By **K'ajji**

NIGHTMARES OF A HUSTLA III

By **King Dream**

THE WIFEY I USED TO BE II

By **Nicole Goosby**

IN THE ARM OF HIS BOSS

By **Jamila**

MONEY, MURDER & MEMORIES III

Malik D. Rice

CONCRETE KILLAZ II

By **Kingpen**

HARD AND RUTHLESS II

By **Von Wiley Hall**

LEVELS TO THIS SHYT II

By **Ah'Million**

MOB TIES II

By **SayNoMore**

BODYMORE MURDERLAND II

By **Delmont Player**

THE LAST OF THE OGS II

Tranay Adams

FOR THE LOVE OF A BOSS II

By **C. D. Blue**

<u>Available Now</u>

RESTRAINING ORDER **I & II**
By **CA$H & Coffee**
LOVE KNOWS NO BOUNDARIES **I II & III**
By **Coffee**
RAISED AS A GOON I, II, III & IV
BRED BY THE SLUMS I, II, III
BLAST FOR ME I & II
ROTTEN TO THE CORE I II III
A BRONX TALE I, II, III
DUFFLE BAG CARTEL I II III IV V
HEARTLESS GOON I II III IV V
A SAVAGE DOPEBOY I II
DRUG LORDS I II III
CUTTHROAT MAFIA I II
By **Ghost**
LAY IT DOWN **I & II**
LAST OF A DYING BREED I II
BLOOD STAINS OF A SHOTTA I & II III
By **Jamaica**
LOYAL TO THE GAME I II III
LIFE OF SIN I, II III
By **TJ & Jelissa**
BLOODY COMMAS I & II
SKI MASK CARTEL I II & III
KING OF NEW YORK I II,III IV V

RISE TO POWER I II III
COKE KINGS I II III IV
BORN HEARTLESS I II III IV
KING OF THE TRAP
By **T.J. Edwards**
IF LOVING HIM IS WRONG…I & II
LOVE ME EVEN WHEN IT HURTS I II III
By **Jelissa**
WHEN THE STREETS CLAP BACK I & II III
THE HEART OF A SAVAGE I II III
By **Jibril Williams**
A DISTINGUISHED THUG STOLE MY HEART I II & III
LOVE SHOULDN'T HURT I II III IV
RENEGADE BOYS I II III IV
PAID IN KARMA I II III
SAVAGE STORMS I II
By **Meesha**
A GANGSTER'S CODE I &, II III
A GANGSTER'S SYN I II III
THE SAVAGE LIFE I II III
CHAINED TO THE STREETS I II III
BLOOD ON THE MONEY I II
By **J-Blunt**
PUSH IT TO THE LIMIT
By **Bre' Hayes**
BLOOD OF A BOSS **I, II, III, IV, V**
SHADOWS OF THE GAME
TRAP BASTARD
By **Askari**
THE STREETS BLEED MURDER **I, II & III**

THE HEART OF A GANGSTA I II& III

By **Jerry Jackson**

CUM FOR ME I II III IV V VI

An **LDP Erotica Collaboration**

BRIDE OF A HUSTLA **I II & II**

THE FETTI GIRLS **I, II& III**

CORRUPTED BY A GANGSTA I, II III, IV

BLINDED BY HIS LOVE

THE PRICE YOU PAY FOR LOVE I II

DOPE GIRL MAGIC I II III

By **Destiny Skai**

WHEN A GOOD GIRL GOES BAD

By **Adrienne**

THE COST OF LOYALTY I II III

By Kweli

A GANGSTER'S REVENGE **I II III & IV**

THE BOSS MAN'S DAUGHTERS I II III IV V

A SAVAGE LOVE **I & II**

BAE BELONGS TO ME I II

A HUSTLER'S DECEIT I, II, III

WHAT BAD BITCHES DO I, II, III

SOUL OF A MONSTER I II III

KILL ZONE

A DOPE BOY'S QUEEN I II

By **Aryanna**

A KINGPIN'S AMBITON

A KINGPIN'S AMBITION **II**

I MURDER FOR THE DOUGH

By **Ambitious**

TRUE SAVAGE I II III IV V VI VII

DOPE BOY MAGIC I, II, III
MIDNIGHT CARTEL I II III
CITY OF KINGZ I II
By **Chris Green**
A DOPEBOY'S PRAYER
By **Eddie "Wolf" Lee**
THE KING CARTEL **I, II & III**
By **Frank Gresham**
THESE NIGGAS AIN'T LOYAL **I, II & III**
By **Nikki Tee**
GANGSTA SHYT **I II &III**
By **CATO**
THE ULTIMATE BETRAYAL
By **Phoenix**
BOSS'N UP **I , II & III**
By **Royal Nicole**
I LOVE YOU TO DEATH
By Destiny J
I RIDE FOR MY HITTA
I STILL RIDE FOR MY HITTA
By **Misty Holt**
LOVE & CHASIN' PAPER
By **Qay Crockett**
TO DIE IN VAIN
SINS OF A HUSTLA
By **ASAD**
BROOKLYN HUSTLAZ
By **Boogsy Morina**
BROOKLYN ON LOCK I & II
By **Sonovia**

GANGSTA CITY

By **Teddy Duke**

A DRUG KING AND HIS DIAMOND I & II III

A DOPEMAN'S RICHES

HER MAN, MINE'S TOO I, II

CASH MONEY HO'S

THE WIFEY I USED TO BE

By Nicole Goosby

TRAPHOUSE KING **I II & III**

KINGPIN KILLAZ I II III

STREET KINGS I II

PAID IN BLOOD **I II**

CARTEL KILLAZ I II III

DOPE GODS I II

By **Hood Rich**

LIPSTICK KILLAH **I, II, III**

CRIME OF PASSION I II & III

FRIEND OR FOE I II

By **Mimi**

STEADY MOBBN' **I, II, III**

THE STREETS STAINED MY SOUL

By **Marcellus Allen**

WHO SHOT YA **I, II, III**

SON OF A DOPE FIEND I II

Renta

GORILLAZ IN THE BAY **I II III IV**

TEARS OF A GANGSTA I II

3X KRAZY I II

DE'KARI

TRIGGADALE I II III

Elijah R. Freeman
GOD BLESS THE TRAPPERS I, II, III
THESE SCANDALOUS STREETS I, II, III
FEAR MY GANGSTA I, II, III IV, V
THESE STREETS DON'T LOVE NOBODY I, II
BURY ME A G I, II, III, IV, V
A GANGSTA'S EMPIRE I, II, III, IV
THE DOPEMAN'S BODYGAURD I II
THE REALEST KILLAZ I II III
THE LAST OF THE OGS
Tranay Adams
THE STREETS ARE CALLING
Duquie Wilson
MARRIED TO A BOSS... I II III
By Destiny Skai & Chris Green
KINGZ OF THE GAME I II III IV V
Playa Ray
SLAUGHTER GANG I II III
RUTHLESS HEART I II III
By Willie Slaughter
FUK SHYT
By Blakk Diamond
DON'T F#CK WITH MY HEART I II
By Linnea
ADDICTED TO THE DRAMA I II III
IN THE ARM OF HIS BOSS II
By Jamila
YAYO I II III IV
A SHOOTER'S AMBITION I II
By S. Allen

TRAP GOD I II III

By Troublesome

FOREVER GANGSTA

GLOCKS ON SATIN SHEETS I II

By Adrian Dulan

TOE TAGZ I II III

LEVELS TO THIS SHYT

By Ah'Million

KINGPIN DREAMS I II

By Paper Boi Rari

CONFESSIONS OF A GANGSTA I II III

By Nicholas Lock

I'M NOTHING WITHOUT HIS LOVE

SINS OF A THUG

By Monet Dragun

CAUGHT UP IN THE LIFE I II III

By Robert Baptiste

NEW TO THE GAME I II III

MONEY, MURDER & MEMORIES I II

By **Malik D. Rice**

LIFE OF A SAVAGE I II III

A GANGSTA'S QUR'AN I II III

MURDA SEASON I II III

GANGLAND CARTEL I II III

CHI'RAQ GANGSTAS I II III

KILLERS ON ELM STREET

By **Romell Tukes**

LOYALTY AIN'T PROMISED I II

By Keith Williams

QUIET MONEY I II III

THUG LIFE I II

EXTENDED CLIP I II

By **Trai'Quan**

THE STREETS MADE ME I II

By **Larry D. Wright**

THE ULTIMATE SACRIFICE I, II, III, IV, V, VI

KHADIFI

IF YOU CROSS ME ONCE

ANGEL I II

By **Anthony Fields**

THE LIFE OF A HOOD STAR

By Ca$h & Rashia Wilson

THE STREETS WILL NEVER CLOSE

By K'ajji

CREAM

By Yolanda Moore

NIGHTMARES OF A HUSTLA I II

By King Dream

CONCRETE KILLAZ

By Kingpen

HARD AND RUTHLESS

By Von Wiley Hall

GHOST MOB II

Stilloan Robinson

MOB TIES

By SayNoMore

BODYMORE MURDERLAND

By Delmont Player

FOR THE LOVE OF A BOSS

Killers on Elm Street

By C. D. Blue

Romell Tukes

BOOKS BY LDP'S CEO, CA$H

TRUST IN NO MAN

TRUST IN NO MAN 2

TRUST IN NO MAN 3

BONDED BY BLOOD

SHORTY GOT A THUG

THUGS CRY

THUGS CRY 2

THUGS CRY 3

TRUST NO BITCH

TRUST NO BITCH 2

TRUST NO BITCH 3

TIL MY CASKET DROPS

RESTRAINING ORDER

RESTRAINING ORDER 2

IN LOVE WITH A CONVICT

LIFE OF A HOOD STAR

Killers on Elm Street